FOUR GHOSTLY TALES

Duncan Wood

Copyright

© Duncan Wood 2012

The moral right of Duncan Wood to be identified as the
author of this work has been asserted
by him in accordance with the
Copyright, Designs and Patents Act of 1988

All rights reserved

Dedication

For Glenda and Susanne
And, of course, Mandy

Lux in tenebris lucet

TABLE OF CONTENTS

MAUSOLEUM	7
ANNELIESE	39
HIGH TOP	69
OUR JACK'S BACK	97

MAUSOLEUM

Edward Dorset put down his mobile phone and picked up his son. He held the child up high above his head and gazed, smiling, into the infant's eyes, giving him the gentlest of shakes.

'You, my boy, are going to be the glory of my house,' cried Edward.

The child, Robin, giggled.

'He'll be sick on you,' warned Edward's countess, Jane.

'Doesn't he have a cherubic face?' remarked Edward. 'His eyes are agleam!'

'You're terribly sentimental for a businessman!'

'But I've gone into business for the boy's sake,' replied Edward. 'After two centuries of falling masonry and dwindling cash, the family's going to be rich again. Young Robin here will be the richest Earl of Dorset that this country's ever seen.'

'I think you're counting chickens, darling.'

'Oh, those two American chaps wouldn't have bought into the scheme unless they thought it was going to yield them a fantastic return on capital.'

'Obviously,' replied Jane, 'but the question is whether they're right. I'm still not convinced that people are going to buy luxury houses next door to a theme park.'

'There'll be a thick belt of woodland between them to stop the noise, and quite different access roads to the two areas. I'm sure this is going to work. I can feel it in my loins!'

Jane laughed.

'What are you going to do about the Mausoleum, though?'

'I haven't decided yet.'

'Well, you can't leave it in the theme park!'

'It's virtually full! We're not going to use it again, are we?'

'Your mother will go berserk if they build a roller-coaster around it!'

'Even the screams of teenage girls couldn't wake these sleeping Earls. And don't you think that hurtling above a bunch of corpses would add a unique twist to the thrill of the ride?'

'Have you no respect for your poor lamented father?'

'Of course I have. That's why I'm restoring the fortunes of his house. Those mouldering remains in the Mausoleum are no more my Papa than the old pipes and tobacco pouches in the bottom drawer of my desk are!'

'But your mother won't see it that way.'

'Mama has no control over the estate.'

'She has control over you, though!'

'Yes, I suppose she could make me miserable if she wanted to. Well, I'll ask Thrill Out's engineers to take a look at the place and see if it can be moved.'

'And if it can't, I'm sure Mother will want you to shift the theme park's boundary.'

'That could cost me a lot of money.'

'You're going to have to decide which is more inimical to your peace of mind, less cash or a dowager's curses!'

'Indeed,' murmured the 13th Earl, inserting his son and heir into a bouncing chair.

Edward turned to gaze thoughtfully over the rolling sunlit parkland of Webham Hall. In the distance, blue-green velvet woods hid the Dorset Mausoleum from view.

***

The Mausoleum was in a clearing on the top of a hill deep in the interior of the ancient woodland that stood to the west of Webham Hall. It was a huge and solemn edifice that brought a gasp of astonishment to the lips of any walker who saw it for the first time from a turn in the path on one of the forested hills surrounding it.

With its Doric columns standing like sentinels at chamfered corners, the square building of Portland stone would have seemed menacingly squat and powerful had it not been for the tall four-sided pyramidal roof. It was enclosed by a wrought iron fence behind which a deep ditch offered further repulsion to the curious. The only obvious access was by a flight of stairs that led over the trench to a massive mahogany door, the solidity and darkness of which forbade the ingress of the living into this realm of the dead.

Rain was just starting to drop when Iain Taylor, Lord Dorset's estate manager, and Bob Cook, the chief engineer from Thrill Out, pulled up in Iain's Range Rover Sport at the bottom of the Mausoleum steps. The two men ran quickly up to the heavy double door.

'It really would have been better if our bosses had sorted this issue out before signing the contract,' commented Bob, in his soft and friendly New Hampshire accent.

'I can't imagine what it would cost to pull this lot to pieces and rebuild it somewhere else,' said Iain. 'His Lordship's going to lose out financially either way, whether he moves the building or the boundary; but if he leaves the Mausoleum in the theme park, then he'll have the Dowager Countess to contend with; and believe me, she's as formidable as a big gun battleship would be to a fleet of fishing smacks when she gets going!'

Iain was struggling to turn the lock. Suddenly, the huge key moved. The two men pushed the doors open slowly. The bottoms of the doors scraped over the stone floor, dragging a thick collection of dead leaves along with them. Some of these were doubtless from ash trees that had sprouted in the entablature above. The Mausoleum was not well maintained.

'What exactly are we looking for?' asked Bob.

'Whatever it is, we won't see much in this gloom!' responded Iain, taking a torch from the pocket of his jacket.

They were standing at the mouth of the funerary chapel. A discreet amber light filtered into the building from high lunettes that pierced the stonework of the east, north and south walls. An altar stood against the east wall, facing them, its reredos a bas-relief sculpture, after Antonio da Correggio, of the Risen Christ saying 'Noli me tangere' to an obviously overwhelmed Mary Magdelen. In front of the altar a marble sarcophagus was oriented along the east-west axis, on top of which coffins were usually laid during the funeral office.

Bob asked how coffins were lowered into the crypt.

'Two methods,' replied Iain. 'The top slab of this tomb-like thing here is removable. It comes away in two halves, which can be laid down on either side of it. The coffin then rests on temporary blocks over the aperture; and at the moment of committal is lowered by bands into the crypt below. Or, less decorously, it can be carried back out of the Mausoleum, down the flying staircase, round the back, down the ditch, and brought back in through the tradesman's entrance. That was done for the 9th Countess. She was too fat to go through the hole.'

'That must have been terrible!'

'It was. One of the pallbearers fell and broke his leg.'

Bob grinned.

'Can you get into the crypt from the interior?' he asked.

'There's a tiny spiral staircase at the north side of the door here. The walls may look like solid stone but they aren't. The whole structure's made of brick, with a stone facing.'

Bob stared up at the domed ceiling that decorated the inside of the pyramidal roof. 'This would be one complex building to pull apart and put together again,' he murmured.

Iain looked up. He was calculating the potential cost of relocation under his breath when he heard, and felt beneath his feet, a dull rumbling and scraping sensation.

Bob glanced at Iain and asked, 'What was that?'

'I don't know,' said Iain, 'but if it's a structural fault, it might make it a bit easier for His Lordship to justify moving the whole blessed pile!'

'I suppose we'd better go and look,' said Bob.

They went to the top of the intramural staircase and, turning on their torches, cautiously made their way down.

The crypt was like a well of black ink. A mere trace of light managed to struggle through a couple of small windows that had been almost blocked by foliage growing outside. Iain and Bob stood at the bottom of the stairs, flashing their torches rapidly around the sepulchre. The space was circular with a shallow-domed ceiling. The walls consisted mainly of three banks of loculi, each bank being four high and four wide. In every loculus but one there was a coffin. In the middle of the crypt there was a marble table onto which coffins were lowered from the funerary chapel above.

They could hear no further sound, apart from the dripping of rain water through the cracked window at the north side. The crypt seemed quiet. The two men carefully searched the walls for any sign of structural failure but could find none.

Iain stopped beside and pointed at a large velvet-clad coffin surmounted by a stamped-iron funerary coronet in a central niche on the eastern side.

'This is the chap who built the Mausoleum,' he said. 'Julius Ferrar Argent, the 3rd Earl, who spent a fortune building it and promptly died a month after it was consecrated by the Bishop of Rochester. That was in 1789. Quite a character was Julius. He held a sinecure post under the government and used the income from it to speculate in stocks. He made a lot of money through his knowledge of government secrets. What we'd call insider trading today.'

'This was on top of the income from his land, I guess?' said Bob.

Iain nodded.

'He made a lot of money, and blew most of it on high living. He believed that that was a rational thing to do. "Eat, drink, and be merry, for tomorrow we die." The irony is that it was probably eating and drinking that killed him.'

'How old was he?'

'Forty eight.'

'Well, not bad for those days, I suppose.'

Bob ran his finger over the plaque on the coffin and read the inscription. 'It is a huge casket!' he said.

'Not as bad as the 9th Countess's over there!'

'Hang on,' said Iain, suddenly. 'What's this?'

Bob trained his torch on the niche that Iain was staring at. 'What's up?' he asked.

'It's the 4th Earl, Robert Ferrar Argent. There's something odd here.'

Robert's coffin was in the same bank of loculi as his father's but one step to the right and one step upwards.

'What do you mean?' asked Bob.

'Look, the coffin isn't in its niche properly. This end hangs over the edge, and it isn't central. It's always been a point of principle here to place the coffins neatly.'

'That goes with the classical architecture, I suppose.'

'This coffin's been shifted to the left.'

Bob read the dates on the 4th Earl's plaque: 1763 – 1793.

'This one died even younger,' he commented. 'What happened to him?'

'He drowned in a riding accident. It was quite a loss to the country. He was a War Minister under Pitt the Younger. They say the First Coalition against the French Republic might have beaten Robespierre & Co if only Robert Dorset had lived. Look here.'

'I'm a bit too short,' said Bob. 'Do you mind if I step up onto this ledge?'

'Go ahead. Just don't put your hands in Robert's niche.'

Bob lifted himself by his right leg and grasped the uprights of the loculus below Robert's.

'Do you see?' asked Iain. 'There's a dust free triangle to the right of the coffin. That must mean that the coffin was moved recently.'

'Perhaps there were some leaves in there that brushed the dust off when the wind blew them around?'

Iain flashed his torch towards the two windows.

'True,' he said, 'there are some leaves on the floor, and both windows are open to the air a little. But that doesn't explain why the coffin isn't central.'

'You're not suggesting that it actually moved while we were talking upstairs, surely?'

'Well, I don't know!'

'I reckon this is all due to the squall of rain outside.'

'A squall wouldn't have moved the coffin.'

'Then maybe it was done by some mortician, years ago.'

'Maybe,' said Iain.
But he was suspicious.

***

That night, after a good dinner in their rambling cottage on the home farm, Iain related the tale of the moving coffin to his wife Gillian. She laughed at his puzzlement.

'Perhaps you've just never noticed the angle of that coffin before?' she said. 'After all, you don't visit the crypt very often, do you? Most of your knowledge of it comes from books.'

Sipping from his excellent cup of Ethiopian coffee, and looking forward to a quiet night of domestic tranquillity, Iain chose not to disagree with his wife.

'Well, maybe,' he said. 'But I'm unwilling to rule out the possibility that an intruder got into the Mausoleum somehow.'

Iain turned on the television to watch a documentary about Schrödinger's cat, and soon become absorbed in the question of whether it was alive or dead, or both. The prospect of the cat being both at once made him shout abuse at the presenter; and Gillian went to bed.

The next morning, Gillian went to the Hall to take some eggs to the kitchens. The Dorsets were entertaining the Lord Lieutenant and several of the county's Conservative Members of Parliament that evening, and planned to serve bread and butter pudding according to a recipe invented by the Prince of Wales. The chef had been instructed to use ingredients – bread, butter, cream, eggs, raisins, brandy – from Lord Dorset's own farms and cellars.

Gillian found the Countess in the kitchen telling the chef how an ultra light pudding would symbolise the light touch of Conservative economic policy. The chef, who was a silent socialist, listened carefully; but he fondled the thick crusts of the loaf beneath his hands.

When the Countess had finished giving her semiotic instructions for the dinner, she turned to Gillian and asked what conclusion Iain had reached after his inspection of the Mausoleum.

'Oh, it depends on the financial modelling,' said Gillian, 'but I shouldn't be surprised if he recommends moving the boundary rather than the Mausoleum.'

'I wonder if there's an intermediate option?' mused Jane. 'We could open the theme park in two phases. The revenue stream from the first phase could help to pay for the relocation of the Mausoleum; and then in the second phase, new attractions could be built where the Mausoleum used to be.'

'I really don't know whether that would work or not,' admitted Gillian. 'What I do know is that Iain's spooked by the whole thing!'

'What ever do you mean?'

Gillian told the curious Jane about the missing dust and about Iain's suspicion that someone had moved the 4th Earl's coffin.

Later, Jane recounted the tale to her husband over lunch in the green dining room.

'What?' laughed Edward, wiping soup from his chin. 'Maybe old Robert doesn't like the idea of a death ride over his head; and wants to escape before we can build one!'

'Gillian said that Iain was brooding about it quite a bit.'

Edward shook his head.

'Oh, it was probably just the undertaker working out how to best to make space for papa last year,' he said. 'Maybe the chap thought about rearranging the coffins and then changed his mind. Iain's just vexed because he didn't know about it. You know what Iain's like. He must be in total command of the detail, or he's as miserable as a violinist with a broken bow!'

'By the way,' said Jane, 'I had a clever idea today about building the theme park in two stages.'

She explained her idea.

Her husband was impressed.

'That might just work,' he said. 'I'll put it to the Thrill Out people.'

***

Despite the hundreds of things that engaged him, Iain could not rid himself of the suspicion that something was wrong at the Mausoleum; so a few days later he drove out there again, to take a second look around - alone.

It was a bright June day with just a few cumulus clouds drifting slowly across the sky. The sun was directly overhead, and its light picked out the Mausoleum, contrasting its light grey stone and straight edges with the dark and sinuous lines of the surrounding woodland.

Iain ran up the stairs and opened the heavy doors without a moment's trouble this time. He switched on his torch and went straight down the spiral steps to look at the 4th Earl's coffin.

'What the hell?'

The coffin was almost half way out of its niche.

Iain ran back upstairs and quickly locked the doors to the Mausoleum. He did not want anyone coming in or going out. Then he went back down into the crypt and set about searching it thoroughly for anyone who might be hiding in its obscure places. Only when he had checked the shadowy recesses did he turn to the protuberant coffin and ensure that it was stable. It seemed steady enough, so he went back up the stairs to probe the funerary chapel for malefactors. Again, he could find nobody.

He returned to the crypt and stared at the misplaced coffin in silence.

'We need to get your Lordship back again,' he said, eventually.

Placing his torch in his pocket, so that its light shone upwards, he placed both of his hands on the end of the coffin and pressed as hard as he could.

The coffin moved back slightly, with a staccato series of creaks, and then shuddered to a halt. No matter how hard he pushed, it offered an equal and opposite resistance. He paused and wiped his dusty hands on a handkerchief. He then pushed again but still the coffin would not budge.

'Maybe there's some kind of structural problem after all,' muttered Iain to himself. 'I wonder if fallen masonry's obstructing the path back into the niche?'

He pondered on what to do.

'I'll have to come back and attend to your Lordship's needs later,' he announced, 'along with a few of my broad-shouldered workmates.'

***

Jane Dorset was in the estate office, asking the clerk to order some more gravel for the dips and holes that had recently opened up in the front drive, when Iain Taylor arrived asking for some men to help him lift down the coffin and remove the rubble that he expected to find behind it.

'Before you do anything, Iain,' interrupted the Countess, 'will you please show me this impertinent coffin? I want to see it with my own eyes!'

'But you've got Lord Webham with you,' protested Iain.

Viscount Webham was the courtesy title of the eldest sons of the Earls of Dorset, in this case the one year old Robin.

'Oh, he won't be intimidated by the place. It'll mean nothing to him.'

'It's not a healthy place for a youngster,' insisted Iain.

'Okay then, I'll ask Gillian to come with us and entertain Robin in the fresh air, while you take me on a ghost tour of this poltergeist-infested crypt!'

'I don't believe in ghosts,' Iain said, shaking his head. 'I'm sure there's a natural explanation.'

'There probably is,' answered the Countess. 'But let me see it for myself.'

***

Iain's torch picked out the protruding coffin.

'It's travelled a lot further since lunch time.'

'It looks on the verge of toppling out!' said Jane.

She stepped into the pool of light and ran her hand over the end of the coffin.

'It's very cold,' she said.

'The whole crypt's cold.'

Jane studied the name plate on the end of the coffin. 'Why does this particular name sound so familiar to me?' she said. 'Maybe Edward has told me some story about him.'

She placed both her hands flat on the end of the coffin and tried to push it back herself. She managed to move it about a quarter of an inch when she suddenly gave a cry and pulled her hands away with alacrity.

'What is it?' asked Iain.

'It pushed back!'

'Surely not?'

The whole vault juddered. Iain and the Countess both grabbed the mortuary table to steady themselves.

'Look out!' cried Iain.

The 4th Earl's coffin was sliding, at an angle, out of its niche.

Jane jumped out of the way.

The coffin stood upright for a moment, facing her, teetering, and then, with what seemed like great deliberation, fell down onto a corner of the mortuary slab, smashing open the velvet-covered outer case at the head, before bouncing back, half spinning, until it landed with a resonant thud, face upwards, on the floor.

Jane and Iain coughed. They grimaced in disgust. Foul gases filled the crypt.

An anxious voice echoed down the spiral staircase.

'Are you okay down there?' It was a worried Gillian.

Nobody answered. Despite Iain's attempt to restrain her, Jane, holding a crumpled tissue over her nose and mouth, stooped and looked inside the ruptured coffin.

'I'm coming down!' shouted Gillian.

Jane peered into the hole that the collision had made in the coffin. With what force must it have hit the mortuary slab? The impact had smashed a hole through the velvet covered outer case, the lead container in the middle, and then straight into the inner coffin of elm wood.

For a second or two, Jane could not detect any pattern in the various shades of grey in the shadowy cavity thus created. Then she gasped. She could see the upper right quadrant of the dead Earl's face; and his eye was open.

'Bring your torch closer,' she beckoned to Iain.

Jane could hear Gillian clattering down the stairs, calling her name from the bottom step, walking up to her. She could hear Robin making his happy 'hello' noise. Yet she could not avert her gaze from the stare of the uncorrupted eye.

'Jane,' murmured Gillian, puzzled, alarmed, taking hold of the Countess's arm.

Jane half turned, and took her son from Gillian's arms.

Mother and child both stared into the coffin.

***

Edward Dorset pressed the play button on his stereo system and the first of Sebastian Bach's 48 Preludes & Fugues for a well-tempered clavier filled the sonic space of the drawing room. His Lordship retreated to his deep yellow arm chair with a sigh of contentment.

'Well, the whole tale's quite a brain teaser,' he said. 'What can have caused the blessed coffin to pop out like that? Was it vibration from the high speed rail tunnel, do you think? Or perhaps the initial ground-works for the Thrill Out park?'

'It could be a ghost,' said Jane, pulling a face of dismay.

Edward laughed.

'Maybe my late ancestor was so proud of his shiny eye that he engineered an earthquake just to show it off to you!'

Jane shook her head.

'I'm sure it's not a ghost, Jane. This is hardly the work of a sentient mind. In fact, it all seems rather random to me.'

'Do ghosts have sentient minds?' queried his wife.

'I don't really know!'

There was a pause.

'I do feel odd,' said Jane.

'I'm not surprised after so ghastly an experience. You say that Iain actually cling-filmed the hole in the coffin?'

Jane nodded.

Edward raised his eyebrows and grinned.

'I must send a plumber and a carpenter up there tomorrow. What a bizarre tale. How on earth was the old boy's eye still intact? The embalmer must have been a wizard!'

'Perhaps it's all down to the RAF,' suggested Jane.

'What, the incorrupt eye?'

'No, you idiot, the movement of the coffin!'

'Oh, you mean the fighter trials? Resonance, and all that? How intriguing. I wish I'd paid more attention to physics at school.'

'Would you mind turning on the fire, darling?'

'But it's June!'

'Please!'

'The pink paint on the walls should keep you warm enough in the summer.'

'You can afford the gas.'

Edward rose from his armchair and turned on a coal-effect fire that stood, rather incongruously, in the old stone fire-place that still survived from the Tudor house.

'Now, where's the Book of Ancestors?' he queried. 'Let's see what it says about the eyeballing 4th Earl.'

Edward went into the great library and, mounting a step ladder to search the middle shelves, found the volume he wanted. It was a leather-bound collection of biographical essays that his grandfather had written about all those Argent men who had adorned their heads with coronets of strawberry leaves and silver balls before him. The old boy had ordered the essays to be printed, with reproductions of various paintings and photographs of all the stern visages, rampant beards and luxuriant moustaches concerned.

'Here we are,' said Edward, returning to the drawing room. 'Why, here's a picture of the man Robert himself!'

'Let me see,' cried Jane, rising eagerly from the Madame Recamier sofa on which she had been reclining.

She seized the book from her husband's hands.

The 4th Earl was portrayed in commanding pose in the House of Lords, penetrating the scoundrels on the opposition bench to their corrupt hearts with his piercing stare.

'Well, do you recognise him?' queried Edward.

Jane nodded.

'Now, how did he die?' asked Edward. 'Shall I read it out?'

This is what he read:

Lord Dorset was at the height of his powers as Secretary at War, and reforming the Army in a way that destroyed privileged inefficiency and promoted soldierly competence, when he himself was suddenly seized by the Angel of Death. Although there were rumours at the time that he might have been the victim of a plot by French spies, this was dismissed by fellow Ministers as an idle invention of tale-mongers. What appears to have happened is that His Lordship had been riding for exercise on the tracks and ways in the woodland of the Webham estate when, at a gallop, he suddenly struck a low bough of a sturdy tree, was knocked, probably unconscious, from his horse, and rolled down the steep bank beside him into the deep waters of Webham Mere, in which he drowned. This, at least, was the conclusion reached by the High Sherriff of Kent, who investigated the matter at His Majesty's express command.

Although the King and his Ministers were desirous of giving Lord Dorset a public funeral in Westminster Abbey, with the rare privilege of burial in that sepulchre of kings, his brother and successor, Wystan, the 5th Earl, and the widowed Lady Dorset, and her young daughter, the great man's only child, all expressed a solemn wish for the deceased's obsequies to be performed in his own church at Webham, and then for His Lordship to be buried in the Mausoleum that had been erected on the family's land by the departed's noble great grandfather as a classical temple to Lucretian resignation in the face of death.

The 5th Earl, a shy and retiring man, nevertheless found the courage to make a heartfelt funeral oration, in which he praised his brother for those remarkable qualities of vision, energy, determination and martial zeal which had made him such a great defender of his country and of his *class against the evils of the Revolution in France. The 5th Earl remarked that he was proud to bathe in the reflected glory of his older brother, though as a quiet and unworldly scholar of the starry heavens, he felt no attraction whatsoever to the excitements of government. The 5th Earl, finally, pledged himself to the give succour to his brother's widow and orphan, as the sacred scriptures and the natural affections of the heart both commanded him to do.*

Edward stopped reading and looked at his wife, who had turned very pale.

'I feel a little unwell,' said Jane.

'What's the matter?'

'I feel rather drained. It's probably just a cold.'

'Perhaps it's shock, darling. You should rest.'

'Yes, I think I'll go to bed.'

They gave each other a tiny kiss of parting.

Jane went upstairs.

Edward remained in the drawing room, reading the Book of Ancestors. He wondered what he could write in new chapters about his father and grandfather. Both had been outstanding diplomats who had exercised a profound influence on the foreign policy of the country. This possible vocation as family historian was so appealing to him that he took his Blackberry out of his pocket and started to tap his thoughts into it.

Three hours later, he went to bed.

Jane was asleep, murmuring uneasily, raising an arm and placing it across her eyes. She looked flushed. Edward gently laid the backs of his fingers on her forehead but was surprised to find that she felt cold.

Jane brushed his fingers from her face and sat up suddenly.

'Edward!' she gasped.

'What's the matter?'

'Oh, I just ... well ... you know?'

'You were having a bad dream.'

'Insects,' said Jane. 'They were burrowing. It was quite nasty.'

'Sounds perfectly horrid,' said Edward. 'Take some brandy to calm you down.'

***

The next day, Iain Taylor took a plumber and a carpenter to the Mausoleum to repair the damage to the 4th Earl's coffin. They travelled in convoy up the forest tracks, as each tradesman had his own tools and materials to take with him to try and get the job finished in one go.

'This is going to be pretty gruesome,' said Iain, as he unlocked the great double doors of the funerary chapel. 'After 220 years of being sealed from the air, His Late Lordship has a lot of decay to catch up on.'

The tradesmen shrugged and followed him down the spiral staircase.

'What the devil?' cried Iain as he stepped off the last turn.

This time, eight coffins were partially pushed out of their loculi, making jaunty angles as their lids caught on the tops of niches.

'Someone's been having a party in here,' said the plumber.

'I smell what you mean,' said the carpenter.

'All Earls, numbers 5 to 12,' said the plumber. 'A men only party!'

Iain was looking down at the 4th Earl's coffin.

'Let's seal this one before we do anything else,' he said.

'What's the damage?' said the carpenter, peering down at the smashed wood.

'I wouldn't look too closely,' said Iain. 'Doing that made Her Ladyship ill.'

'Well, I can't see anything at all,' said the carpenter.

'Neither can I,' said the plumber, shining his torch straight into the cavity.

Iain forced himself to take a close look.

'Well, blow me,' he exclaimed. 'It's empty!'

'Rotted away overnight?' suggested the carpenter.

'Surely not,' said the plumber, 'there must be something in there still.'

The two men lifted the coffin upside down and shook it vigorously.

'Have a look inside now,' the plumber said to Iain. 'Is there anything there?'

Iain went down on hands and feet and looked into the hole with his torch.

'Not a thing,' he said.

'What do you want us to do then?'

'God knows. I think this is a job for the police.'

***

Chief Inspector Rabett stroked his unfashionably long beard.

'Well,' he said, glancing around the crypt for the tenth time, 'I don't think this is a job for the police. There's no indication that any crime's been committed here. There are no signs of a break in through any of the windows or doors. The only marks of violence are the dents and cracks in the coffin of the 4th Earl; and as you say, Mr Taylor, you and Lady Dorset saw that one fall out of its niche, unaided by human hands, with your own eyes, making those very same marks that we see now. And now the 4th Earl's body has completely vanished. But there are no further marks of forcible entry on the coffin. I doubt that anyone's opened it further.'

'Could someone have opened it and resealed it?' asked Iain.

'I doubt it,' said the Inspector. 'See, the velvet cladding of the outer case just hasn't been touched. You can see that from the way the dust is evenly spread over it. All the stitching is as ancient as you could wish for. I reckon it's just a case of rapid decomposition, Mr Taylor, after sudden exposure to the air; but I will ask the lads at the forensic science lab for a second opinion, to make sure, though I'm pretty certain I'm right.'

'Well,' said Iain. 'Is it okay for my colleagues here to repair the damage now?'

'I don't see why not, once SOCO's gathered a few samples of this mortal dust.'

'Good. I just want to get the crypt back to normal as quickly as possible.'

***

Jane Dorset was sitting at the small desk in the great library of Webham Hall, reading the Book of Ancestors for herself. She shivered as she read the story of the 4th Earl's drowning. She picked up her notebook and wrote:

'I could almost feel the cold waters of the lake closing over my head, my hopes and fears thrashing in a semi-conscious moment as I sank, then the agonising search for breath that would not come.'

Jane closed her notebook and glanced towards Robin, who was sleeping on a sofa near her. Reading of sudden death had made her realise how easily the soft fabric of life could be ripped apart. She spent a few minutes watching her son's gentle, regular breathing. The lulling rhythm made her feel drowsy herself and she began to doze.

The library clock struck four and Jane woke with a start.

A shadowy figure was bending low over Robin.

Jane screamed.

The figure turned towards her. It was wholly grey and featureless but she could sense eagerness in its pose.

Jane's scream woke Robin and he started to cry.

Edward rushed into the room from his study.

'What is it?' he cried, picking up his son.

'I don't know,' said Jane.

'What do you mean, you don't know? You almost shattered the windows!'

'I thought I saw something.'

'What?'

'A figure bending over Robin. I'd just woken up, though.'

'What kind of figure?'

'Oh, I don't know,' she said. 'It was just a shadow.'

'A shadow of what?'

Jane hesitated.

'A cloud?'

'You must have been dreaming.'

'I expect so.'

The couple looked at each other in silence for some moments.

'Edward, is it you who's doing those things at the Mausoleum?'

'To be quite frank, I wondered if you were?'

'Why would you suspect me?'

'You've played rather a bigger part in the story so far than I have.'

Jane shivered.

'Robin feels cold too,' said Edward. 'Come into the drawing room. We can snuggle in front of the fire together.'

'I'd like that.'

'I'm going to clear out the Mausoleum if it's the last thing I ever do.'

***

The Rector struggled to light his cigar.

'Bless me!' he exclaimed. 'I can scarcely keep my hands steady.'

Edward grinned at him and held out a match. This time the end of the fine Cuban cigar – 'rolled on the thighs of some dusky woman,' as Edward's father had been fond of saying – acquired and kept a bright red glow.

'You're shaken by what I'm asking,' said Edward.

Secretly, he thought that the Rector had indulged a little too much in the Chablis over lunch.

'Well, it is it quite a revolutionary proceeding, my Lord,' said the clergyman.

'There is something spiritually diseased about the place,' said Edward. 'Something has disturbed the rest of the dead. Surely, it's our duty as Christians to return them to their rightful slumbers?'

'I'm sure that's true,' said the Rector, turning crimson as cigar smoke found its way up his nose and into his ears. He coughed violently.

'Do have a drop more wine,' said the Earl, pouring a medicinal quantity into the Greek scholar's glass.

'Thank you,' spluttered the Rector. 'Being Christian is one thing. Being an Anglican is another. I'm sure we'd need a faculty from the Bishop and quite possibly an exhumation order from the Home Office. And doesn't the Mausoleum have listed building status? Goodness me, I'd hardly know where to start.'

'Start with my father and work back to the 1st Earl.'

The Rector smiled thinly. Had his interlocutor not been a peer of the realm, the good man might have retorted with a waspish remark.

'But where could I put all of their Lordships' remains? Not to mention their Ladyships, who not infrequently require more space than their Lordships do?'

'I'd be very happy for them all to rest in some sunny corner of the Webham churchyard extension,' replied Edward. 'That seems to me to be a far healthier resting place than the now rather volatile Mausoleum!'

'Well, I suppose so,' said the clergyman. 'But it does use up a lot of our new burial space in one go. I'm not at all sure what the parochial church council will say.'

'Surely, their minds are on higher things?' queried Edward. 'They're still collecting for a new bell, aren't they?'

'Why yes, they are,' said the Rector. 'The great number six bell cracked after we tried to ring a full extent for Her Majesty's jubilee; and we're desperate to replace it.'

'You know, my father loved the bells of Webham church,' mused Edward. 'I'm sure he'd want me to help out. That way, he could enjoy them as he lies in his garden of sleep in Webham churchyard.'

'By St Michael and All Angels,' said the Rector. 'That would be most fitting.'

'Good,' said Edward. 'We're agreed then? You'll persuade the church council and I'll attend to the necessary licences. I'll have a quiet word with the Bishop in the House of Lords next week. He's hoping for my vote on the Pornographic Advertisements Bill. And if necessary, I'll give the Home Secretary a call too. Or is it the Justice Secretary these days?'

'It seems a shame to dismantle the Mausoleum,' murmured the Rector. 'It's such a fine piece of neo-classical architecture. As a sepulchre, I believe it be second only to Hawksmoor's splendid edifice at Castle Howard. I can't help feeling that to move it from its romantic sylvan location would weaken the contrast that the architect intended. Don't you think so?'

'It won't be destroyed,' said Edward, avoiding the aesthetic question. 'I can assure you of that, my dear

Rector. What I can't guarantee, though, is that it will stay in this country. I believe that I have a buyer for it in California.'

'How distressing!' said the Rector. 'It will be used as a wine cellar.'

'Not as distressing as it's proving to be here for my unhappy wife,' said the Earl. 'Tell me, Rector, do you believe in ghosts?'

The clergyman began to cough over his cigar again. He believed that ghosts were merely tokens of psychological disorder in the people who experienced them, but did not want to say that to the Earl about his countess. Fortunately, Lord Dorset lost track of his question in pursuit of a glass of water.

***

This was the next entry in Jane's notebook:

'I must have a virus. My energy is disappearing to no obvious place. It does not matter how well I eat or drink, or how long or deeply I sleep, I constantly felt weak and tired. The sharp reality of daily life has become blurred and drained of colour. I want to do very little and can do less. I have an immobilising sense that below the conscious stream of my mind, something very menacing, over which I have no control, is coiling itself up. Am I going mad?'

As she slowly brushed her hair in the dressing room mirror, Jane's glance moved around the room, in front of, beside and behind her. This constant searching had become a habit over the last four weeks. She was nervous of any momentary shadow that flitted across the room, as, for example, when a cloud eclipsed the sun.

Robin was sitting in a playpen beside her. Jane noticed that Robin's gaze kept returning to the same corner of the room, the one behind her on the right. He was smiling and holding out his left hand from time to time, as if asking for something. She studied the corner carefully through the mirror for some minutes, and then turned round to look directly.

There was no sign of anything untoward in the corner. There was no mysterious shadow that borrowed the lineaments of human form.

She got up from her seat at the dressing table and walked over to the corner to take a closer look. A hard chair stood across the angle of the room. Clustered on the walls on either side of it were miniatures of her mother and father, her brothers and sisters, and a few cousins. Jane glanced at them but was distracted by a sudden shriek of laughter from Robin. She turned and looked at him.

'What's amusing you?' she asked.

A miniature suddenly struck Jane on the shoulder, making her yelp. It rebounded onto the chair and finally clattered to a standstill on the wooden floor.

Jane picked it up. The cover was smashed. The portrait had been badly gouged by a large shard of glass; but she could see from what remained of the face that it did not belong to any member of her family. She read the name at the bottom of the oval and saw that it had been a portrait of the 5th Earl of Dorset, that quiet scholar of the starry heavens.

Jane looked at the wall in cold puzzlement. All the miniatures of her own family were still there.

***

'Okay,' said Iain Taylor. 'That'll do for today. We can move the rest tomorrow.'

Only the first four earls and countesses were left in the Mausoleum. Over the space of the previous week, all the more recent ones had been moved and reburied in what

Edward called the 'good clean earth' of the newly extended Webham churchyard.

An environmental health officer was there to ensure that no physical pestilence could escape from any of the coffins.

'What are you going to do with this one?' he asked, tapping the newly repaired coffin of the 4th Earl. 'You say it's empty?'

'Well, let's say it was less full the second time I looked into than it was the first! But I didn't stick my hand in to rummage about for bones either.'

'I can't blame you,' said the health officer. 'As the copper said, the corpse probably just turned to dust once you exposed it to air.'

'I dare say. But most of His Lordship's crumbling remains should still be in there.'

'The rest of the coffins are airtight,' said the health officer, 'which is just as well, as I'm a bit worried about why Lady Dorset's been so ill since she looked inside this one.'

'The blokes who mended the coffin have been fine,' commented Iain. 'On the other hand, Lord Webham's been a bit under the weather. Did you speak to Her Ladyship's doctor in the end?'

'He says it's probably a virus. He's sent off bloods for testing.'

'Between you and me,' said Iain, lowering his voice, 'I reckon it's psychological.'

'But why should the breaking of the coffin have affected her so much?'

'Well,' said Iain, with a shrug, 'that's a mystery, as the Rector would say.'

Iain suddenly clapped his hands.

'It's time to go home, everyone! We'll meet here again at 1 pm tomorrow to remove the last eight. Thank you all very much.'

***

Edward woke up with a shout from a dream in which the coffins of his ancestors were ablaze in the Mausoleum. Sweat was pouring from him. He felt as if he were on fire himself.

'This is what comes of drinking claret instead of burgundy,' he muttered.

He reached out to see if he had disturbed Jane. She was so quiet that he thought perhaps he had not woken her. His hand felt around her side of the bed. Then he realised that she was not there.

He sat up and turned on the bedside lamp.

'Jane?' he called, softly, looking around the room.

There was no answer.

Edward clambered out of bed and went to see if Jane was in Robin's room next door. The room was empty. The bedclothes in Robin's cot had been pulled back.

Alarmed, Edward rushed out onto the landing and raced down the great staircase. He ran to the library where Jane had been spending so much of her time recently. The lights were on; and the Book of Ancestors was open on the desk; but neither Jane nor Robin was there.

An idea sprang into Edward's brain. He ran down the back stairs and into the key room beside the butler's pantry. His eyes quickly scanned the rows of keys.

'Damn!'

The key to the Mausoleum had gone.

Edward knew immediately that that was where Jane had taken Robin. Ever since she'd gazed on the paper-like face of the 4th Earl, Jane had become more and more obsessed with the idea that this long dead man, Robert Ferrar Argent, was trying to communicate not only with her but with her son. She had not said so directly and had even denied it outright when Edward had confronted her with the idea; but he could see no other reason why she was constantly reading or talking about or gazing at paintings of his ancestor.

Edward ran back to his bedroom. Pulling on his dressing gown and slippers, he grabbed his keys and dashed out to his Land Rover in the courtyard of the Hall. Within a minute, he was sweeping across the gravel. He turned onto the drive that led past the house, and raced out across the dark parkland. The woods that shrouded the Dorset Mausoleum hurtled towards him in the beam of his lights. His stomach was full of fear. Jane would try to break into the coffin of the 4th Earl again. He felt sure of that. She was obsessed. He pressed the accelerator as hard as he dared. He must stop her before she could expose their son to any more corruption.

Once inside the woods, Edward sped along the level track beside Webham Lake. He was just turning the bend to begin the long climb to the Mausoleum when, to his horror, he saw Jane standing, startled, in the path of the car - with Robin in her arms. He stamped on the brake. But his wife and son were too close. Blocked in by oak and elm to the right, Edward threw the vehicle sharply to the left and yanked up the hand brake.

The vehicle began to spin. It flung itself over the verge, careered down the steep bank of the lake, and hit the water like a great ship on a slipway. Within seconds, it sank beneath the surface. The lights shone in the darkness of the water for what felt to Jane like a suspense of time; and then flickered and went out.

Robin made a gurgling noise in his throat and giggled.

Jane took her mobile phone from her pocket and dialled Iain Taylor.

***

Chief Inspector Rabett took off his glasses and polished them carefully before returning his scrutiny to Jane's face.

'So you can't explain why you chose to go for a walk in the woods in the middle of the night?'

'No,' said Jane, 'I'm afraid I can't. I'm not even sure that I was awake. It was either a random thing to do, or ...'

'Or what?'

'Perhaps I had a subconscious motive that I wasn't aware of.'

'Where did you think you were going?'

Jane paused and reflected.

'I sensed that I was going somewhere that would reveal an answer to the turmoil of the last four weeks.'

'But you didn't know where?'

'Well, part of me thought that I would learn more if I returned to the Mausoleum, but that didn't seem important after I'd been walking for forty minutes or so. And although I was on the path to the Mausoleum, I just turned back and thought of my bed.'

'Did you feel that you'd got your answer at that point?'

'No, I don't think so.'

'Why did you take your little boy with you?'

Jane shrugged her shoulders.

'It just seemed a natural thing to do,' she said. 'I'm a hands-on mother, Inspector.'

'Unusually among the nobility. How come you didn't ask Lord Dorset to go with you?'

'He was fast asleep, snoring heavily. He'd had a lot of wine.'

'You didn't want to wake him?'

'I felt that I shouldn't.'

'What did you do when saw the car's headlights?'

'I walked towards them. I was attracted by the light.'

'And when you rounded the bend in the track and saw the car right on top of you?'

'I froze. I couldn't see. The sudden glare of light was painful.'

'So what happened?'

'You know what happened. Edward swerved to avoid us.'

'You think he chose to protect you and the boy at risk to his own life?'

'I doubt if he could have gone into the trees without turning the car on top of us.'

'So he steered into the lake instead?'

'Yes.'

The Chief Inspector curled the ends of his moustache absent-mindedly.

'Would you say that you found the illumination you were seeking?'

Jane smiled thinly and shrugged her shoulders again.

'But you no longer feel as ill as you did a few days ago?'

'No. That's very strange. I feel a lot better. And so does Robin.'

***

Jane was in the great library reading Burke's *Brief Life of Robert, 4*th *Earl of Dorset*, and making notes in her pocket book when Price the butler announced Edward's mother.

The senior dowager was a tall, slim, woman in her late fifties who somehow managed to combine elegance with athleticism. Her medium length grey hair was pulled

36

back and held in place by a silk band, giving her face a distinctly lean and ascetic appearance.

'Mama,' said Jane, rising and kissing the older woman.

'Jane.'

This was not an encounter that either of them had been looking forward to.

'I'm so sorry,' said Jane.

'Why do you say that? Was it your fault?'

'It was an accident.'

'So the Inspector told me.'

'There was no helping him.'

A brittle silence ensued.

'Have you begun to think of the funeral yet?' asked the older woman.

'I suppose you'd like Edward to go in the Mausoleum?'

'I certainly would not,' said his mother.

'Where then?'

'He should be buried with his dear Papa in the churchyard.'

'Do you not want to save the Mausoleum?'

'I did.'

'But no longer?'

'I think I'd like to see it destroyed now.'

'But it's part of our family's heritage.'

There was another silence.

'I assume,' said Edward's mother, 'that you do not propose to ship back into that wretched crypt all the corpses that my son removed from it?'

'Oh, no. I think we should just leave the remaining bodies there.'

'The first four earls?'

'Yes.'

'I see you've been reading Burke's *Brief Life of Robert*.'

'Yes. I have to say he's a fascinating man.'
'I take it that you know?'
'Know what?'
'That you're descended from him?'
Jane played with her wedding and engagement rings.
'I had forgotten until very recently,' she murmured.
'Through his only daughter.'
'My father told me years ago, when we first moved here, when I was a child.'
'You must have remembered at the time of your marriage, though?'
Jane shook her head.
Edward's mother sniffed.
'Robin is the 4th Earl's direct descendant,' said the older dowager.
'But Edward wasn't.'
'No. Edward was descended from the 5th Earl.'
'From Robert's brother, Wystan.'
'Who was found with Robert's drowned body at the exact spot where you were found with Edward's.'

ANNELIESE

It all started when my sister died. She was only fifty six. She had had mysterious abdominal pains for over two years and had been losing weight. At first, the doctors said that she had a hernia; which was true. What they failed to detect, however, was that she also had advanced pancreatic cancer.

I sat by Brenda's deathbed for as long as I could find the courage. I held her hand and she held on to mine. That was her way of saying farewell. Or at least, I think it was. She did not admit, at least to me, that she was dying. She pretended to have a long afternoon ahead of her still. But really she knew that darkness was about to fall. She died quietly, in the middle of the night, amid the comforts of palliative medicine and a loving family.

What I mourned most of all was the loss of someone with whom I had shared all the excitement and promise of childhood. Does that sound selfish? Naturally, I grieved for the extra years of life that unruly cells had stolen from Brenda. But it was the stark contrast between the glorious morning of her childhood and this now finished life, irrevocably in the past, which shocked me most.

For many days after Brenda's death, I could hear her soft rounded voice, getting quieter and quieter as time went by, but still plainly audible, asking me what I was going to do to give a good account of my own life before that too would be over. Her premature death became for me a challenge not to waste any opportunity that I had been given or could still have.

Do not misunderstand me. I am not talking about Brenda's ghost. I did not believe in life after death. The voice I heard was one of memory and imagination. Yet it was a powerful voice and I heeded it.

**

The first thing I did was to try and make contact with all the friends I had lost over the years through my own neglect.

Facebook proved quite effective for tracking down men. Frankly, however, it was useless for locating women, most of whom had presumably either married or divorced. Some of the women I found by writing to other people with whom I guessed they might still be in touch. In a few cases, I searched for them on Google in the slight hope that their names would give some leads.

There was one woman in particular whom I was very keen to find. I had met her in Sweden at an international youth conference in 1977. In those days, I was a tall, gauche, skinny, unkempt, ill-attired student. Yet I was on the look-out for an attractive girl with whom I could fall in love. And I mean 'love'. Sex in those days seemed rather an ugly thing to me. I was much more interested in romance. There were several girls at the conference who had the power to thrill a boy's heart but one, Anneliese, was as beautiful as a Mozart piano concerto.

Looking back, I wonder whether this was because she was so young. She was sixteen and I was nineteen; and she had a freshness and brightness that was entrancing. This was not the carnal desire of an older youth for a younger girl. I would have been delirious had I simply been able to hold her hand. I felt like a medieval knight worshipping his unattainable beloved.

You may laugh, but I was also attracted to Annaliese because she was German. This was the first time that I had ever been abroad; I knew that the German people were a formidable nation; and this made me very curious about them. Germany was a pillar of the two things that mattered to me most in life: science and music. This was the nation of Bach, Mozart and Beethoven, of Planck, Einstein and Heisenberg.

Anneliese seemed to bear out the notion that the Germans were a nation well-stocked with blonde hair and blue eyes; and yet with some variation, for her hair, which was beautifully thick and luxuriant, was fair rather than blonde; and her eyes, which were grey-blue, always had a curious watchfulness about them.

The only words of German that I knew had been picked up from childhood comic books about the Second World War. When pressed by my new-found German friends to say a few words in their language, I could only shout 'Hande hoch, Englischer schwein-hund!', to their immense amusement. Anneliese could slowly string together basic English sentences but that was infinitely more than I could do in 'die deutsche Sprache'.

Despite the fact that we knew so little of each other's language, we seemed to resonate emotionally. We were happy in one another's company. We communicated more through looks, smiles, gestures, pointing, and just being able to enjoy walks in the beauty of the Swedish countryside together, than through words. Anneliese remarked on this herself in her published reflections on the conference.

Do I need to tell you that I was soon in love? Yet I was far too timid to tell Anneliese that I desired her. I was daunted by the doubly difficult task of finding the right words.

Anneliese asked me, at the end of the festivities, whether she could sit next to me on the coach that would take us back from the small Swedish town of Malmköping to Hamburg. I was so elated that I almost floated away over the lake like a hot air balloon. But, as we sped through the forests of Sweden on our way to the Malmö ferry, I did not dare to take her hand.

Of course, I wanted to kiss her when, eventually in Hamburg, we parted, she setting off for Berlin and I for Rotterdam; but again I did not dare.

When I got home to England, the first thing I did was to write to Anneliese and ask if I could go and see her in Berlin. She replied quickly saying that of course I could - as long as I didn't mind sleeping in her tiny little room.

After a few weeks at home in Lancashire, I went back to Cambridge and picked up the threads of my applied mathematics degree. I was trying to master Dirac's bra-ket notation for quantum mechanics at the same time as pondering the far more difficult question of how to declare my love for Anneliese.

I was finally inspired to be brave one night by Mozart. I was sitting at my desk in college, gazing out over the dark graveyard beyond my window, listening to the great man's Sinfonia Concertante in E Flat on my plastic record player. There is a passage in the first movement in which the violins lead the orchestra, with growing boldness and excitement, in a thrilling ascent of some high mountain of desire; and this resolved me to declare myself.

I picked up my pen with passionate determination to win Anneliese but could only bring myself to write 'Du bist sehr schön'. I went out glumly into the chilly night and thrust the letter into the post box just outside Pembroke over the road.

In those days, student grants were generous and I saved up a lot of money to buy an air ticket to Berlin. However, I allowed my father to dissuade me from going. His arguments were dull ones about the cost of travel and, in view of how quickly I might outstay my welcome with Anneliese's family, the cost of accommodation. It now seems incredible that I was dissuaded by this essay in pessimism. Young men should always disregard at least two-thirds of what their fathers say.

How I wish that I had seized my chance to go and see Anneliese in Neukölln, the suburb of Berlin where she lived, before her life was so cruelly stopped.

Anneliese was keen to travel before going to university. She spent many months working in the United States. Then, to my surprise, she wrote in 1980 asking if she could come and stay with me for a few days while she toured the United Kingdom on a rail pass.

I accepted with pleasure. I persuaded my employer, a nuclear engineering company, to give me a week off at relatively short notice. I tidied up my little terraced house in readiness. I decided to give her my bed and I would sleep on a sofa in the front room downstairs.

I returned home from work one day to find her sitting on the doorstep. I remember very clearly the searching look she gave me as she rose to her feet and held out her hand.

Anneliese and I enjoyed nearly a week exploring the living idylls of Lancashire and Yorkshire. I regaled her with tales of the Wars of the Roses. She can hardly have understood them. I listened with uncomprehending pleasure to her German as she chattered excitedly over my telephone with her family in Berlin. In the evenings, we ate and drank with friends in some of the liveliest pubs of Oldham.

Walking home one night, I told Anneliese how nice it was to see her again. She said it was nice to see me too. Then we walked on in silence.

Annaliese decided to take the sleeper to Inverness and see the Highlands. I took her to Werneth station and waved her off. As the train pulled away for the run down to Manchester Victoria, we just gazed at one another. Her thoughtful face grew smaller and smaller. That was the last time I saw her alive.

***

When I started to look for Anneliese, I assumed that my search would probably fail. I thought that in all likelihood she would have married and had children; and that with a new name she would be unreachable. Certainly, a careful trawl of Facebook caught no fish. As a final effort, I searched her name on Google. This found a few women with the same name but they were much younger. However, one document did seem promising. My German was still not good but this was some kind of official report, dating from the early 1980s, and Anneliese's name was mentioned in it. But I soon realised that it was a report on violence against women. Next to her name I saw the word 'gemordet'. This alarmed me. I knew enough German to know that this meant murder. I cut and pasted the text into an online translator which gave me the outline of the story. I started to search for more details to check whether this poor girl was indeed my old friend. I was aghast at what I found. Newspaper articles about the killer's trial left no doubt that this was indeed my Anneliese. I cannot bring myself to repeat the horrifying details here. All I can say is that this mysterious and beautiful woman had suffered a lonely, vicious and painful death one November night in Berlin. When I saw a grainy photograph of the place where she had been killed, I closed down the window as if it were radioactive.

***

When my wife Ruth came home from work, I told her what I had discovered.

Naturally, Ruth was shocked to hear that someone whom I counted as a friend had met so cruel a death. However, I had never mentioned Anneliese to her; and so Ruth had no real sense of how emotionally significant the dead woman had been to me. She soon launched into a story about how one of her enemies at work had tried to claim credit for her ideas on a new depth psychology course.

I searched for Anneliese's old letters to me in the cupboard in my study. I had not read them for years. There was a letter from 1977 in which she breathlessly said that she had never received a letter from outside Germany before; and that she had had to buy air mail paper and envelopes specially to reply.

Later letters talked of my visiting her in Germany; or of her trying to get a place on a youth conference in Britain; or of taking up a place as an au pair girl in Germany; and then of working in a hospital in Berlin to see if she wanted to be a doctor, and deciding that this was not a life for her; and of deciding to study European literature at university instead. She was a student of literature when she died.

I suddenly remembered that somewhere I had ciné footage of Anneliese, walking towards me along a jetty on the lake beside the conference centre in Malmköping. This was only a fragment because, annoyingly, the film had become loose on the spool in the standard 8 camera that I had borrowed from my father; and when I tried to extract it, sitting in the dark in a pantry with the camera on my lap, the door had been opened by someone, spoiling the film with the light. Still, there was a watchable fragment.

I quickly found the film in a cupboard and retrieved Dad's old projector from the attic. To my relief it still worked, and in my darkened study I projected the flickering, light-damaged, heavily blotched image onto the large whiteboard I use for writing out equations.

I could see Anneliese sauntering towards me with a smile and quizzical eyes. It was like looking through a tunnel in time and seeing her alive again. Tears welled up in my eyes. I had hoped that I might be able to meet her again after all these years; but a conspiracy between human depravity and the laws of nature had obstructed me.

Yet Anneliese and I had once been able, mysteriously, to communicate with one another, despite the fact that language was almost an impermeable membrane. Perhaps physical death, like language, was not a total barrier?

I had long since abandoned any faith in a personal god or in comfortable notions of life after death. On the other hand, I had never believed that mental events are reducible to physical ones. There is an ocean of difference between the conscious experience of seeing a red rose, and the electromagnetic radiation that enables one to see it.

As I watched the cloudy images moving on the whiteboard for the second, third and fourth times, I implored Anneliese, if she still existed in some place that was nowhere, and in some moment that was beyond time, to make herself known to me; though I had not the faintest idea of whether or how she might be able to do this.

***

I went to bed that night feeling exhausted. I read a few pages of a biography of Max Born, the mathematician who invented the probabilistic approach to quantum mechanics - who as a Jew had to flee Germany in 1933, on top of being usurped for the Nobel prize by the young Werner Heisenberg - but fell quickly into a deep sleep.

I woke suddenly in the small hours. Immediately, I felt impelled to look towards the half open door of the bedroom. An unearthly grey-blue light shone there and in that light I sensed, rather than saw, the presence of a human figure. I tried to focus my eyes so that I could see this figure more clearly, but I could not. The apparition was not one over which I had any physical purchase at all. Indeed, it gripped me. I felt confused and paralysed. Then I felt immense terror.

With a desperate effort, I struggled to an upright position and forced myself to wake fully. I started to sob. I was convinced that Anneliese had been standing at the door of my bedroom, looking at me. And yet I had no reason other than this conviction itself to believe that somehow my dead friend had visited me.

My sobbing woke Ruth. She asked me what the matter was. She put her hand on my arm. I mumbled something about crying for Anneliese and turned over. As soon as Ruth had fallen asleep again, I turned back and stared through the doorway. All I could see was the hazy grey-blue light that came from our wireless network router on the landing.

Had this light somehow evoked a memory of Anneliese's watchful eyes? I did not want to believe that she had actually answered my call, for the answer did not reveal a soul that was at rest.

***

I did not really believe in ghosts. True, I had asked Anneliese to reveal herself; but in the clear light of day I soon came to regard that invocation as the flower of a sentimental moment. After two cups of strong and sugary coffee, I dismissed my nocturnal experience as the misfiring of a tired brain. I did not expect any further visitations. Indeed, I was quickly absorbed by more earthly matters.

You see, I was tormented by a choice I had to make. I had to choose between two living women. On the one hand, I had my wife, Ruth, a secondary school psychology teacher, to whom I had been married for nearly twenty five years. On the other hand, there was Cathy, a colleague at the university, an economist, with whom I had been having an affair for the last year.

How on earth had I got myself into this situation?

I now wonder whether my relationship with Ruth had supernatural origins. I say this because when I was doing my PhD at the University of Manchester's Institute of Science & Technology, the librarian, who was as sour a person as you could ask for, suddenly said, as Ruth and I waited for our books to be stamped out, 'Surely, you two will end up married!' Yet that queue was the very first place that Ruth and I had ever encountered one another.

The prophecy certainly came true. Ruth and I suited one another very well. We had broadly similar views. We wanted much the same lifestyle. We had sufficiently overlapping interests to enjoy one another's enthusiasms; but also allowed each other plenty of space for activities that the other found boring. I always found Ruth physically attractive. Ruth never said much about my looks. When I grew a beard, her only comment was that it made me look less ugly. Nevertheless, we soon had a common interest in raising our two sons. We liked the same holiday destinations and musing around old churches and castles. But over the years, Ruth became just too familiar. There was no creative disturbance. There was no volcanic activity, physical or mental, just the occasional gentle bubbling of a thermal spring.

Cathy, on the other hand, was an elemental force. I'm not entirely sure what she saw in me. The word 'victim' comes to mind. She was a dogmatic, imperious, intellectually astute but politically infuriating right wing economist. Whereas I read Voltaire and listened to Mozart, she read Nietzsche and listened to punk rock. She was taller than me, stronger than me, more confident and self-assertive than me. She believed that human beings are born with differing skills and abilities, and that the sum of human happiness depends on giving the most able free rein to do more or less what they like.

Cathy was exciting and funny to be with, and refreshing among economists, because she was much more interested in the reality of power relationships than in the idiocies of the general equilibrium theory of markets. For a right winger, she was quite a Marx scholar, praising the sharp insight of his early work in the *Economic & Philosophical Manuscripts*, but pouring scorn on the 'mathematical wanking' of *Das Kapital*. She ridiculed Ruth's favourite psychologist, the mystically-minded Jung, and instead praised Freud as a man who looked unflinchingly at the harsh realities of human motivation.

What attracted me most to Cathy was that she blew like a fresh wind that would rescue me from intellectual doldrums. Frankly, I had become stale as a physicist. My early hopes of doing creative theoretical work had been dashed. I just did not have the imagination. It pains me to be so candid about this; but it is true. I then turned to applied physics and the art of quantum cryptography. I will spare you the underlying mathematics, but quantum entanglement, the strange phenomenon in which very distant things can have instant effects on one another because they were once part of the same system, enables the sender and receiver of a message to share an unbreakable code. This was exciting work for a while but still left me feeling more like a mechanic than a creative thinker.

Provocatively, Cathy had encouraged me to apply my mathematical skills to Ruth's discipline of psychology. She had read a magazine article about how quantum entanglement is much better at explaining experimental results on human memory than classical psychological explanations such as 'spreading activation', in which links between two distant ideas are made in a series of small steps through a large network. Here, she said, was an exciting and important new area of work in which I could make my mark.

Inevitably, Ruth found out about Cathy. I had tried to hide the affair but Cathy had been quite open about it. Typically, she thought there could be no real progress in any of our relationships until there was a period of creative destruction among them. Cathy was happy to share me with Ruth, but Ruth was not happy to share me with Cathy.

My own strategy was to play for time. I did not know whether I preferred the beautiful gardens of a country cottage or the rugged grandeur of a snow-clad mountain. I thought that perhaps events would reveal which of these I should choose.

I hesitate to confess my duplicity; but I must, if you are to understand the story that I am about to tell you. On the one hand, I had to pretend to Cathy that I was as wild and free as she was, otherwise she would hold me in contempt as someone who is shaped by society rather as someone who shapes it. On the other hand, I had to pretend to Ruth that I was being torn in half by the lure of two loves, all the time trying to balance, like the considerate fellow that at heart I was, the interests of two very different but equally needy women.

I knew I had to make a choice; but I did not want to; and I tried to evade the choosing.

But Cathy understood the true situation.

'You, Gordon,' she said to me one day, coolly watching me put on my boxer shorts inside out without saying a word to correct my mistake, 'are like Buridan's ass.'

'Remind me.'

'Buridan's ass was a donkey that died of thirst and starvation because it didn't know whether to eat the bale of hay on its left or drink the pail of water on its right.'

I laughed.

'Haven't you noticed that I'm doing both at present?'

'Actually, you donkey, it's you that's being eaten – and from both sides.'

***

It was the end of August. Ruth wanted us to go away. She was especially keen on this because Tom and Jack, our twin sons, who were both away at university even during the vacations, and usually absorbed by the unscholarly delights of student life, had unusually agreed to go away with us. But I refused.

'I'm sorry,' I said, 'I've got to finish this paper on cognitive entanglement before the new term starts. I just won't have time afterwards. You know how important it is.'

Ruth was incensed. I had never heard her shout so much. She had booked a house in the Pyrenees, near Bagnères-de-Bigorre, for two weeks. I said she should go anyway. She insisted that I should go with her. I was obstinate. 'Business before pleasure' was what, I said, my father had always taught me. She snorted at this, but went, taking her mother with her, and prevailing on Tom to help with the driving.

'And don't expect a postcard!'

Naturally, I took this opportunity to see Cathy. We went out for a couple of meals and I spent one night with her at her flat; but I did not go again. This was not merely due to prudence. It was partly because I wanted to get on with my work; but I was also getting a little tired of Cathy's constant polemics in favour of free enterprise and against welfare. I believed in rewarding the vigorous, as she did, but not in starving the languid. Not even Cathy's exquisite personal geometry and voluptuous voice – going to bed with her was like being shagged by the Jupiter Symphony - could compensate for so many sordid diatribes.

I therefore returned home the next morning with the firm intention of staying there in splendid isolation. In the natural pauses of my work on quantum cognition, I gazed out of the window at the silver birch trees in the garden and thought about Anneliese. I wondered what might have happened to us had I taken that opportunity in Oldham, so many years ago, to give her a kiss as we walked down Doughty Road on our way back from the Lamb & Flag.

How I wished I had been to see her in Neukölln. I berated my long dead father for talking me out of going. I thought of Mozart's journey to Berlin and his writing of the Prussian Quartets, allegedly for King Frederick William II. Constanze Mozart, who'd been left behind in Vienna, was jealous of her husband. After all, he was annoyingly vague in his letters to her about exactly what he was doing where, with whom, and when. For much of the time, he seemed to be accompanied by the singer, Josepha Duschek. Like his biographer, I recognised the signs of a wandering fancy.

I had the Prussian Quartets on vinyl somewhere but no longer had a record player, so I downloaded them from a website. I listened to them through headphones while I wrote my paper on entangled cognition. I fell in love again with the quartets instantly. They were for two violins, a viola and a cello, which last had the most beautiful *cantabile* part. What's more, the quartets conjured up a vision of how my relationship with Anneliese might have developed, had I only ignored my father and gone to Germany.

In the first movement of the D Major quartet I could hear the delight of a young woman exploring a foreign country for the first time, making new friends, tossing back her head to laugh aloud, sweeping her hand across the back of her head to bring her luxuriant dark blonde hair under control. The music unrolled one poignant thought upon another, memories of a bus full of happy youngsters rolling down tree-lined roads, of tired but delighted chatter, dancing, teasing, of beauty shining in the midst of earnest debate and silent moments of longing.

The final two movements of the last quartet in F Major were visions of what might have been had I actually taken that flight to Berlin: cheerful exploration of this lively city; comment and response growing ever easier; the happy but wary building of an emotional charge between us, fluttering uncertainly from time to time; and at the last, hurtling along on bicycles, sure of one another, wheels rolling, wind in our hair, freedom, joy and then skidding to a sudden halt.

The music was too much. I wept.

I could not see to insert mathematical symbols into my draft paper, so I walked along the corridor to the bathroom and ran some cold water into the sink.

I bent over the sink to splash the water onto my face.

I quickly stood up again with a cry. I could see, reflected in the still surface of the water, Anneliese's cool grey-blue eyes, locked on my own.

How could that be? I forced myself to look into the water again. This time, I could see only my own face.

My heart was pounding. Perhaps the Prussian Quartets had over-excited my imagination. I dipped my face into the water, dried myself on a hand towel, and went back to work.

I spent the rest of the day, including the whole of the evening, trying, without much success, to make progress on the first draft of my paper. When I went to bed, I read a few more pages of the Max Born biography but soon turned off the light to sleep.

I was very tired. Within a minute, I was barely conscious.

It was then that I heard a few chords played on the piano in the living room downstairs.

I sat up instantly. Had I imagined the sounds?

I got out of bed and went downstairs, turning on a light as I passed each switch.

The keyboard of the piano was uncovered. Had I left it like that? Or had Ruth? We both played the piano. It was one of the things we enjoyed doing together.

I could not remember whether the lid had been open or not. I turned off the light and went back to the stairs.

As my foot touched the first tread, I heard the piano again.

This time I recognised the phrase. It was the opening of the first prelude from J S Bach's *Well Tempered Clavier*. The hairs began to bristle on the back of my neck.

This was a tune that Anneliese and I had played together on the piano in the salon of the Swedish conference centre.

I stood dithering at the bottom of the stairs. In the end, scientific curiosity prevailed, and I went back to look at the piano again.

This time the lid was closed. Had I closed it a moment before? I could not even remember that, I was so tired. I fixed a piece of sticky tape over the keyhole so that I would know in future if anyone tampered with the piano.

I went back to bed; but not before grabbing all the protection that science could offer against the intrusions of another world: the bedside lamp left on, headphones playing *The Art of Fugue*, and a huge tome on integrated cognitive architecture open on my knee.

I stayed like that, sitting upright in bed, focused remorselessly on how tensor calculus could enable rule- and-symbol reasoning to emerge from non-representational neural networks, for the rest of the night.

I must have fallen asleep at some point, for I awoke late the next morning to the sound of the postman hammering on the front door. I pulled on a dressing gown and ran down stairs to take a parcel from him. It was a book for Ruth.

I was hungry. Opening the fridge door, I searched for anything that would make for an interesting meal. There were plenty of eggs and some mushrooms.

Mushrooms! Immediately, I was back in Sweden, walking with Anneliese in the shade of a pine forest. In the darker places, she was picking wild mushrooms, eating them there and then, and laughing at my refusal to touch them. I just did not trust her knowledge of fungi.

I fried the mushrooms and made an omelette. It tasted good. I threw some hot coffee down my throat and then went into the living room to read the morning paper for a few minutes. I eyed the piano suspiciously. Its lid was still closed and the small piece of tape that I'd attached to it was still there. This was a small victory for science.

I sat down to read the finance pages. I'd invested quite a lot of money recently on Cathy's advice and I was keen to keep abreast of economic trends. There was nothing of much interest, apart from diverse revolts by shareholders against the remuneration policies of their boards of directors. Who was weak and who was strong in this case? I decided to taunt Cathy with this conundrum.

I yawned, stood up and set off in search of a bath.

I didn't get very far. I fell flat on my face. I stumbled over a pile of books that had been left by the settee.

How I cursed. I had not seen them there before. They were Ruth's books. I picked a few up and flung them around the room. Then I paused.

It was most unlike Ruth to leave things lying around when she was going away. She could be obsessively tidy.

So what were these books doing here? Had they been there the day before?

I picked all the books up, threw them on to the sofa; and sat down to look through them.

The first was *Either Or* by the Danish philosopher Søren Kierkegaard. It was not a book that I had read before. It is a strange collection of essays and letters purportedly written by several people. The gist is that one can choose to live either as an aesthete, enjoying beautiful people and things, or ethically, honouring the commitments one has made throughout one's life. The book extols Mozart's opera, *Don Giovanni* as the greatest work of art ever created. I heard in my mind's ear that angry scene in which the statue of the Commendatore, who had been killed by Don Giovanni for defending his daughter from the seducer's attentions, sinks slowly through the earth, dragging the unrepentant Don down into the fires of hell.

The next book was by Carl Gustav Jung, one of Ruth's favourite psychiatrists, whom Cathy describes as a smiling buffoon. What struck me most about this book was Jung's story of how his house was once invaded by a crowd of ghosts. When Jung asked them what they wanted, they all cried out, 'We have come back from Jerusalem where we found not what we sought.' The spine of the book was broken and it opened naturally at a page on which Jung had written about the Anima. This is, apparently, the female part of a man's soul, which man must integrate properly into his Self. I laughed and threw the book back onto the floor.

The rest were worthy but dull books by Aristotle and a mound of other dead people on moral philosophy. It looked as if Ruth had been planning to preach a sermon.

I picked the books up and crammed them back into the bookshelves on the wall of the living room. There were spaces for the books but I found, to my surprise, that I had to shove really hard to get them back in.

Finally succeeding in restoring the twelfth book to the shelves, I rubbed the dust off my hands and turned to go upstairs and dress.

I had just put my hand on the knob of the living room door when there was a loud crack behind me and a thunder of falling books. I spun round in astonishment.

The whole shelving system had collapsed. The three vertical metal strips had come away, rawl plugs, screws and all, leaving gaping holes in the plaster, and a tangled pile of shelves, brackets, metal and broken books on the carpet.

I swore. I did not have the time to repair this mess. I just left it and went back to writing my paper on quantum cognition.

***

I was leaning back in my chair, thinking hard, when I heard a hammering on the door. I tried to ignore it but the hammerer would not stop. Opening the door, I saw Cathy.

'What are you doing here?' I asked.

'I felt like a break from work.'

Cathy followed me back to my study and sat at my desk, flicking through the windows on my laptop.

'This all looks boringly technical, she said.

'Do you mind?'

'I feel thirsty, Gordon.'

I went to get her a glass of water from the kitchen. When I returned, she was not in the study. I found her lying naked on Ruth's side of the bed.

'I was being metaphorical,' laughed Cathy, 'but I'll have it.'

I handed Cathy the glass and noticed that there was a single red rose and a single white rose lying crossed over each other in the middle of the bed. She watched me examine them.

'Very romantic, Gordon,' she said, with a grin.
'You knew I'd come, didn't you?'
'Did you bring these with you?'
'Don't pretend,' she replied. 'I can see what you're saying. Red for you; white for me.'
I was from Lancashire, Cathy was from Yorkshire.
'I didn't put these here,' I said.
'I suppose the cat brought them in from next door's garden?'
'I can't think of a better explanation.'
'Are you asking me to marry you?' asked Cathy.
'No! One marriage in a lifetime is quite enough, thank you.'
'Perhaps there's going to be a death in the house,' suggested Cathy.
'Why do you say that?'
'There's an old superstition that red and white flowers together signify impending death.'
'Do you mean 'death' in the seventeenth-century sense?'
'Oh, you mean la petite morte? I've always found that a strange metaphor for orgasm.'
'So have I.'
'In any case, I mean real death.'

***

Cathy loved to smoke in bed. This was something I hated but was I prepared to put up with it in homage to her sexual virtuosity. I therefore put a cracked old dish on Ruth's bedside table so that Cathy could stub out her cigarette ends in it.
I suspect that the fumes from Cathy's cigarettes explain why I slept so badly that night, even though I had opened the windows wide to allow smoke to escape.

I had fitful disturbing dreams. I can remember this one:

I was sitting on a train with Anneliese. She had a book on her lap. She was flicking through the pages. As she flicked the pages one way, I could see an animated picture on them. The picture was of a man watering and feeding a plant. The plant grew and blossomed beautifully. Then she started to flick the pages in the reverse direction. This time there was an animation of a man walking from painting to statue to painting, with a glass of wine in his hand.

We arrived at the station, where there was a flower shop, and a bar.

'Which one?' I asked Anneliese.

She shook her head.

'I must go down the road.'

'I'll come with you,' I said.

We stepped out of the station into the cold and darkness. I shivered.

'Go and get your sweater,' she said.

I had left it on a bench between the two shops. I retrieved it in a moment.

But when I returned, she had gone.

I looked up and down the long street, but it was empty.

I woke up in horror. Sunlight was coming through the window. Cathy was already out of bed and dressed. The room still stank of stale cigarette smoke. I flung the curtains open so that the air could circulate more easily. I picked up the glass of water and took it back downstairs but forgot the dish of cigarette stubs. Cathy had put it on the floor just before she went to sleep, and I overlooked it.

Cathy was not in the kitchen but I could hear her whistling in my study.

I popped my head around the door.

'Ah, here you are,' I said. 'What are you up to?'

'I'm reading your paper. It's very dull. You should write something that grabs people by the balls, Gordon.'

'Well, this will, if it totally transforms cognitive psychology,' I said.

'Can mathematics really describe things that are emotionally important?'

'I don't see why not.'

'Justify that statement.'

'It can produce models of biochemical systems; and that's what emotions are.'

'I'm still not convinced.'

I glanced at the white board and saw that someone had been erasing bits of my equations.

'Did you do this?' I demanded.

'Do what?'

'Make bloody big holes in my formulae!'

'Of course I didn't!'

I stared at the board and suddenly realised that all of the mathematical terms that had been wiped out were ones using the letters a, n, l, i, e and s; in other words, the letters that made up the name Anneliese.

I must have turned pale, because Cathy asked me if I was alright.

I sat down at my desk and tried to close the file Cathy had been reading that contained my draft paper on cognitive action at a distance. For some reason, the computer kept chiming and showing a message that said 'Word cannot complete the save due to a file permission error'.

I cursed Cathy roundly.

Cathy looked at me curiously.

'I'll go and make some coffee,' she said, and went downstairs.

I managed to close the file without any difficulty by using the mouse instead of the keyboard. No damage seemed to have been done. Perhaps I just needed a new laptop.

While I was waiting for the coffee, I opened the folder that contained the Prussian Quartets folder and clicked the 'Play All' icon.

My blood ran cold. I know that is a cliché; but it is an accurate one.

Instead of Mozart's delightful music, all I could hear was screaming; desperate, terrified screaming; but not of any recognisable individual human voice; it was as if all the suffering of all the creatures in the world had been joined together in a tormented choir.

If you prefer a scientific view of things, a virus in my laptop had joined together all the sounds of pain and agony that it could find on the internet by adding Fourier series.

I did not take the scientific view. I fainted.

I came round to find Cathy pouring brandy over my lips.

'Are you ok?' she asked, looking worried. 'What was that awful sound?'

'How the hell should I know?' I snapped.

'You've not been electrocuted?'

'No, I'm fine. I'm just tired. I slept badly last night.'

Cathy giggled. 'So did I.'

'I think I need to rest. Why don't you go?'

'You're sure you're ok?'

I nodded.

Eventually, after pouring coffee down my throat, she went.

The first thing I did was delete the Prussian Quartet files.

I went downstairs to the piano, broke the sellotape seal, and played the passionate C Minor prelude from the *Well Tempered Clavier*.

I stopped half way through and said to myself, 'I must go to Berlin.'

***

I had found out where Anneliese was buried from her sister.

I had hesitated to write to this woman. I had never met her. My first contact had been with the pastoral office of the church to which Anneliese had once belonged; and I had asked them not to cause any distress to my dead friend's family. In response, however, I received an e-mail from her sister Gisela. Now I wrote back saying that I wanted to visit. I told her when I would reach the cemetery; and she said she would arrange for someone to be there to let me in. The graveyard gates were normally kept locked.

I studied the location of the cemetery using street view on Google maps. On every corner, I noticed a young woman, her face obscured, looking at the camera. It could have been Anneliese as she was as thirty years ago: petite, fair-haired, dark blue jeans.

I texted Ruth to say I was going to Germany for a few days.

Going to Berlin. Will be back soon.
Going to some strip joint with Lucrezia Borgia?
On my own.
Oh, really?

Then I had a text from Jack.

Dad, how come you can go away with her and not us?

I held my head in my hands.

***

I landed at Berlin Schönefeld airport at 8 am and quickly made my way by taxi to the Neukölln district. As the driver was taking me there, I realised that I had not specified which gate of the Evangelischer Gottesacker I would go to.

The driver dropped me off in Friedrich Engels Platz. I quickly found the black-painted solid gate. Over it on some wrought iron work stood the words 'Ich weiss dass mein Erlöser lebt'. I recognised these as the text set so beautifully to music by Handel, 'I know that my Redeemer liveth.'

In a moment, I was transported back to the sun-filled, mellow-panelled, softly-carpeted lounge in Malmköping, asking Anneliese whether they sang *The Messiah* in Germany like we did in England. I could see her again, nodding.

The gate to the cemetery was locked. I tried the handle several times. I thumped on the metal, hoping that someone inside might unlock it and let me in. Nobody did.

I knew that there was also an entrance on the other side of the graveyard, from a small road called Friedhofstrasse. I gave up my thumping and walked round to the back entrance. Or was it the front entrance? I had not noticed on Google. The gate looked just the same but over it this time there was a different text: 'Christus ist mein Leben, Sterben mein Gewinn.'

I gulped. 'Christ is my life; to die is my gain.' This was a hard text for a young woman from whom the full working out of her earthly life had been ripped by violence. I felt a momentary surge of anger – at what, exactly, I could not tell you.

An old man was unlocking the gate. I coughed behind him. He turned and looked at me curiously.

'Ich bin Englisch,' I said apologetically. 'Kann ich den Friedhof sehen, bitte?'

He looked at me steadily from his watery eyes for what seemed like ages. I guess he was trying to process my eccentric German.

'Ich muss das Grab von Anneliese Schneider besuchen,' I explained.

The old man nodded.

'Wilkommen,' he said, and stood aside to let me pass.

I went through, glad that I had learned a bit of German since meeting Anneliese.

I looked around the cemetery. The sun was shining. The air was cool and clear. It looked rather beautiful. The graves with head stones seemed to be clustered along the edges; but most of the ground was laid to grass. There was a touch of dew still in the shady corners. Otherwise, the place looked bright and green.

The cemetery was not very large but I was still worried that it would take me hours to check all the graves one by one. The old man had disappeared somewhere so I could not ask him for help. However, I had two clues. First, I knew that given the customs of the church to which Anneliese had belonged, she was highly likely to be buried under a small flat rectangular stone, bearing only her name and dates. Second, I knew that she had been buried in the early 1980s and therefore I should look for graves of that decade. I assumed that they would be clustered by time.

I started with the flat stones. I went along the rows, reading off names. After a few rows I began to feel dizzy and started to wander around at random. That seemed crazy, so I went back to doing a systematic search.

Within a minute, I had found the grave.

It was just a small stone set into the lawn. I opened my bag and pulled out the red and white roses that had mysteriously appeared on my bed back in England. I crouched down and laid these on Anneliese's stone. This, however, did not seem right. The flowers obscured her name. I moved back a little and lay them, diagonally crossed, on the grass. Having placed them there, I remained squatting before the grave in silence for a few moments; but this was not a comfortable position and I slowly sank forwards onto my knees.

I suddenly felt myself pulled up strongly by hands that had taken hold of my arms from behind. I rose to my feet and turned round. It was the old man. Though ancient in days, he was pretty muscular. He patted me on the shoulder as if to reassure me.

'Sie koennen nicht ihr hier umarmen,' he said. 'You cannot embrace her here.'

He wandered away.

I turned back to the grave with tears forming in my eyes. Again I could not see properly. As I fumbled in my pockets for a handkerchief to dab my eyes with, I noticed the growing scent of a perfume that I had totally forgotten but which instantly signalled Anneliese's presence. And then, through my streaming curtain of tears, I could make out the shimmering form of a young woman with golden hair, red and white striped top, blue jeans, looking at me. I rubbed my eyes frantically with the dirty bit of linen; but the scent faded quickly; and when I could see again, nobody was there.

Some birds flew overhead. I could hear people laughing in Friedrich Engels Platz. There were smells of coffee and kebabs coming from somewhere.

I walked away from the grave feeling that Anneliese had not finished with me.

***

I stayed for a few days in Neukölln to explore the places where Anneliese had lived. While I did this, incendiary texts started to arrive on my mobile phone.

There is a cigarette burn on the bedsheet, you bastard.

This was followed by another.

Bowl of fag ends under my side of bed. This is the end.

I decided to retaliate.

Nearly broke my neck tripping over your bloody books.
Shame you didn't. Why were they on the floor?
The shelves fell down when I tried to put them back.
Sure Wonder Woman wasn't climbing up them?
Tripped over a pile of your books before the shelves fell down.
What books?
Kierkegaard, Jung, Aristotle, other crap.
On shelves when I left.
Why did I trip over them, then?
Because you can't walk straight.

***

On the flight back to England from Berlin a woman came and sat beside me. She was about the same age as me.

I glanced at her slyly. She noticed this and smiled back. She was reading a book in German. I wondered if she looked like how Anneliese would look if she were still alive today. She was about the right build. She had the right hair and eyes. Was she Anneliese?

I shifted uncomfortably in my seat. I looked in the cabin window beside me to see if I could see those searching grey-blue eyes. I could not. All I could see was cloud. I turned around and on a sudden impulse touched the woman's arm to see if she were made of solid flesh. She was. She withdrew her arm hastily and glared at me.

'I'm sorry,' I said, turning red, 'I thought I saw a spider.'

***

The boys were disgusted with me and had cleared off back to their universities, leaving Ruth to fulminate alone at home. She was deeply affronted, as one might expect, to discover that Cathy had slept with me in our marital bed. I cursed myself for allowing that to happen.

Ruth was convinced that I had been cavorting in a week long Dionysian orgy around and about Berlin with Cathy; and that I was only coming home to take both my leave and my suits.

'Why do you want to destroy everything we've built up over twenty years?' she cried.

She ran out into the garden. Had it been day time, I'd have thought that she was going to mow the lawn, which was a favourite form of therapy for her. As it was dark, I imagined that she would try to gather some consolation from the cold impersonal beauty of the starry heavens.

I sat down and put my head in my hands, wondering how to make her believe my story; and, when she eventually believed it, how to make her forgive my indelicacy in our bed.

But she came back with a petrol can and stood in front of the embers of the fire.

'What are you doing?' I asked, uneasily, the palms of my hands beginning to sweat.

'If our home means so little to you,' she said, 'you won't mind watching it burn.'

'Don't be crazy!' I shouted. 'You could kill us both.'

She shook her head and unscrewed the lid of the can.

'I'm sure you can run away quickly enough,' she said, scornfully.

I could smell the fumes.

'It will be a fresh start for us both,' she said.

Ruth turned to face the fire and swung the petrol can back.

'No!'

I leaped up from the settee to grab the can but Ruth had already begun to scream.

I flung my hands in front of my face thinking that she must have set fire to herself.

Then I realised that I could feel no heat.

I opened my eyes and looked.

Anneliese was standing in front of the fire, her left hand on the petrol can, holding it away from the fire, and locking Ruth's hand in its arc of flight.

Ruth stood there, shaking, terrified.

Anneliese's cool grey-blue eyes were on mine, searching.

HIGH TOP

What follows is the text of a lecture given to the North of England Parapsychological Society by Dr Crispin Norton in May 2009.

I have to say that the story of the haunting of 'The Broken Staff' provides very little reliable evidence for survival of bodily death. It is, however, a salutary lesson in how not to conduct a psychical investigation.
First of all, I should tell you where 'The Broken Staff' is. It is a very ancient inn, first mentioned in parish records in 1562, situated between the villages of Delph and Denshaw on the Pennine hills of Saddleworth in Greater Manchester. Here I must ask my Yorkshire listeners to forego their habitual protests about the theft of this part of the West Riding by grasping Lancastrians in 1974. I am a scientist. I am merely recording the facts of this case; and whether the good people of Yorkshire like it or not, Saddleworth is now in Greater Manchester. What is more interesting is that 'The Broken Staff' stands not on the road in the valley between Delph and Denshaw, but almost six hundred feet higher, at the end of a winding lane of incredible gradient in places, in a minuscule hamlet – High Top - right on the edge of Black Peat Moor.
I had visited this public house once or twice before it came to my professional attention. As you can imagine from its location, it is not a tavern that has many casual callers. Its strongest season by far is the summer, when the people of Oldham, Halifax and Huddersfield will drive up there to enjoy a drink or two in the open air in the cool of the evening, while marvelling at the spectacular views over crag and vale. The odd hill-walker or two also calls in for a pint of Old Particular before descending back to the

Accrington brick terraces of Oldham and other such places. Indeed, that is how I first discovered 'The Broken Staff' myself. My second visit was on a dark winter's night for a Christmas dinner of the East Lancashire George Formby Society. The inn was charming then, with its low lights and two roaring log fires, its tankards of hot-pokered ale, and its serried ranks of men playing ukuleles. I was so moved by this homage to one of our greatest Lancastrians that I actually stood up and sang his immortal song 'When I'm growing Rhubarb' myself.

'The Broken Staff' came to my attention professionally about a year ago when I received a telephone call from a Mr Tony Cropper of the 'Oldham Evening Gazette'.

'Is that Dr Crispin Norton?'

'It is.'

'This is Tony Cropper at the Gazette. I understand you're an expert on ghosts, Dr Norton?'

'Do they exist, Mr Cropper?'

'I was hoping you'd tell me.'

'Ah, I'm an expert on the tales people tell about them; but whether they actually exist ...'

'Oh, I see. Well, that'll do me. I'm investigating a haunting at 'The Broken Staff' at High Top in Saddleworth. Do you know it?'

'Indeed I do. What is the nature of the case?'

'Well, the usual, you know, shadows and whispers, things that go bump.'

'I see.'

'I wondered whether your Unit would look into the case?

'Perhaps. I'll have a word with my committee and get back to you.'

It does not do to show too much interest to a potential client. One has to maintain a face of scientific reserve. I am employed by the University of Oldham to teach computer engineering and I'm sure that the dean of my faculty would take a dim view if I pranced around the district giving credence to every superstition and fairy tale I encountered. I keep an open mind on the issue of ghosts, spirits and personal survival; and I have not yet encountered any evidence that would persuade me to close it.

I wish I could say the same about my committee. I make these remarks in total confidence, of course, for fellow members of the Society, who, I know, will share my scientific concerns about amateur ghost-hunters. The truth is that my committee has only one other member, Miss Agnes Mildew, who, in addition to being a writer of romantic fiction and an occasional medium, is extremely wealthy and prepared to fund my research.

'Agnes,' I said, when I telephoned her. 'The local paper's been on to me about a haunting at 'The Broken Staff' at High Top. They want us to investigate it for them. Naturally, I have some reservations. Newspapers always have improper motives.'

'Who doesn't?' cried Miss Mildew. 'The thing, Crispin, is to learn how to make a silk purse out of a sow's ear, whether the sow likes it or not. Do you know the place?'

'I've been there twice.'

'Then you should know that it is a place that resonates with spiritual vibrations from The Beyond,' chided Agnes. 'I'm only surprised that the Whither of All Things has not summoned us there before.'

Thus it was agreed that we should pay a visit to the High Top.

***

The landlord, Bill Buckley, was a surly fellow with a long beard and an aggressive waistline. The first thing I noticed was that he resented our presence.

'What a load of crap,' he shouted.

Then he dropped the glass he was polishing and swore violently.

Tony Cropper, the reporter, and the landlord's wife, Belinda Buckley, seemed very friendly: with us; and with each other. Agnes Mildew and I interviewed them in the Snug. I took the precaution of recording the whole exchange, though Agnes managed to erase it later; so unfortunately I am relying here mainly on memory and a few contemporaneous notes.

'Tell us what you have experienced,' I said to Belinda.

'Using all your senses,' interposed Agnes. 'Smell is the most powerful.'

'It's funny you should say that,' replied Belinda. 'One of the first things I noticed that seemed strange was the scent of lilies. There wasn't a flower in the house, but everywhere I went – lilies.'

'Tell them about the singing,' urged Cropper.

'Yes, I sometimes hear a young woman's voice singing hymns, in the cellar, and once or twice in the old church over the lane as well.'

'When do you hear this?' I asked.

Belinda shrugged. 'Early evening, usually,' she said.

'I dare say,' broke in Agnes, excitedly, 'that there's a tunnel of some kind between your cellars and the crypt of the church. There often is in these cases, you know.'

I groaned inwardly.

'What hymns?' I asked.

'Oh, you know, the old ones.'

'I'm not a church-goer, Mrs Buckley.'

'I think you said it was "All people that on earth do dwell"?' prompted Mr Cropper, the reporter.

'Yes, that was the one,' nodded Belinda.

'And don't forget the shadows,' reminded Cropper.

'Yes, sometimes, a shadow falls on the wall of the lounge,' said the landlady, 'even when nobody's standing between the window and the wall.'

'What about somebody standing between the sun and the wall, but outside?' I asked.

Mrs Buckley and Mr Cropper both laughed.

'Oh, Dr Crispin, you're teasing me!' said Belinda, with a wink. 'But you're forgetting the whispering I can hear when nobody else is the building. Mr Cropper's heard it too.'

Mr Cropper spluttered a little in his beer mug but nodded vigorously.

I went to see Bill Buckley to ask him what he thought about all this.

'A load of cobblers,' he said.

'So you've experienced nothing at all?'

'No, I haven't.'

'Do you believe that your wife has?'

'I'm sure she experiences lots o' things I know nowt about.'

I gazed at him curiously.

'If folk want to come here and see boggles, I don't care,' he said, 'as long as they drink beer while they're doing it.'

***

'What do you think?' asked Agnes Mildew, while we had a private case conference by the gate of the disused All Souls Church just across the lane from the pub.

'I think it's a tale concocted for publicity,' I said. 'They want to drum up trade for the summer. It's April now. If this tale gets in the papers, and appears to have secured our interest, they'll be flooded with curious visitors, all buying beer, bangers and mash.'

'Oh, you're being too harsh,' said Miss Mildew. 'I don't think they're so desperate for business, do you?'

'But look how shabby the place is. The wallpaper's scuffed and torn. And it's peeling off the walls in places. The paintwork is cracking up outside. I'd say they're broke, wouldn't you?'

'I'd say it's moorland chic myself,' Agnes replied. 'The thing that strikes me most about this case, Crispin, is that there's no underlying story. What happened here to cause a haunting? We don't know; which means that we still have everything to find out. You know what we need, don't you?'

I nodded reluctantly.

'A séance?'

'Exactly!'

***

I looked out through a small mullioned window at the back of the closed and silent inn. The vast shapeless moorland behind was dark and forbidding, an expanse of mystery, illuminated only by the feeble rays of a few struggling stars and a waning moon.

'I'm not happy about this,' said Belinda. 'Think of all the custom we're losing by closing for a whole night!'

'But consider all the custom you'll get when Mr Cropper publishes the story that I'm sure we'll discover tonight,' reasoned Agnes Mildew. 'Oh, I can sense it in my ears! They always blush before a successful sitting.'

Mr Cropper nodded. He could see the pecuniary advantages in this exercise.

'Well, I'm not taking part, you silly cow,' said Bill, knocking back a straight whisky behind the bar.

I wasn't clear whether the cow was Agnes or his wife, though I know which one was more bovine in my estimation.

'You get out of there, Bill Buckley, and come and sit round this table,' ordered his wife, her facial muscles displaying a degree of resolution that would have done honour to a gladiator.

'I have no intention of taking part in this nonsense.'

'Well, if you don't, I'll make sure you're on unbroken bar duty for the next year,' retorted Belinda.

Bill muttered curses under his breath. I could see that he was in no position to bargain. He depended on the public house, unsuccessful though it was, for his meagre livelihood; and his wife was evidently a far more effective manager than he. I could imagine that the normal course of things was for Mr Buckley to lurk and glower in the cellar or kitchen, slowly drinking away his pain and rage, while the smiling Mrs Buckley displayed a bright and warming bosom to all comers at the front of house.

'This is a scientific experiment, Mr Buckley,' I said. 'You need have no fear of taking part in anything foolish.'

'How do you mean?'

'Well,' I explained, 'I've set up a range of data capture devices that will show us if anything unusual happens. You can see the video camera there. These machines here are infra-red cameras, controlled by this computer. They can detect significant movement in complete darkness. The computer then angles and focuses them for the best results.'

'What about these bathing caps?' muttered Mr Buckley.

'Ah, they do look like bathing caps, I grant you,' I said, with a chuckle, 'but in fact they're very sophisticated devices of my own invention, called - and this is rather a mouthful I'm afraid – eco-neuro-psychological interaction detectors.'

'Bloody hell,' whispered Belinda Buckley.

'Ridiculous devices,' snapped Agnes. 'I'm sure they'll interfere with the spirit of the séance. All that scientific suspicion would deter even the most ardent communicator.'

'No more than the mental scepticism of sitters like Mr Buckley does,' I calmly retorted.

'How does it work?' asked the said landlord.

'Well,' I explained, 'the caps measure the voltage changes associated with electrical currents in your brain. The spatial pattern of those voltage changes is interpreted by a program in that computer over there to see which brain regions are most active. Using our knowledge of neuropsychology, we can then interpret whether you're seeing or hearing something or perhaps feeling a certain kind of emotion.'

'A crude instrument,' said Agnes Mildew.

'True,' I replied, 'it can be hard to specify the brain region; but some data is better than no data. I'd prefer to use magnetoencephalography but that requires a large machine like a hospital scanner. Anyway, that was the neuropsychology. At the same time, the computer's taking a series of measurements from the environment: air pressure; humidity; temperature; levels of light and other electromagnetic radiation; and the electrical conductivity of a range of natural and artificial substances.'

'A fishing trip!' exclaimed Agnes.

I shook my head and said: 'The final step is for a program to calculate statistical correlations between the neural measures and the environmental measures.'

'But what does it prove?' asked Mr Cropper.

'It will prove either that your reported experiences match what's going on in both your brains and your environments, or that they don't.'

'And which is better?'

'The one is no worse or better than the other. One result would show that your experiences are purely mental. The other would show that they are also physical. We'd then investigate differently according to which result we get.'

'So complex,' commented Miss Mildew with a condescending smile. 'Now, if you're quite ready, doctor, let's begin the séance.'

Agnes Mildew forbade me to sit at the computer control panel and demanded that I should join the circle. We sat in the public lounge around a light and collapsible circular table that Agnes Mildew always brought with her for these events. There were six of us: Belinda and Bill Buckley; Tony Cropper and an old man, Tom Mumpus, who lived in a rather run-down old cottage across the lane from the pub; and Agnes and myself.

The room was utterly dark apart from the flickering glow of my computer screens, which Agnes veiled by draping her thick woollen overcoat over them. She insisted that we should all sit quietly and think of keyholes, and then synchronise our breathing with hers. This was difficult because Tom Mumpus emitted a variety of eccentric wheezes and rattles as a result of a lifetime of smoking unfiltered cigarettes, but after several minutes of rigorous drill even his pipings and trillings fell into line. Then we sat, all breathing as one, each of us with both of our hands on the table, each hand touching a neighbour's, for several minutes.

'Are you there, Napoleon?'

This was Agnes invoking her spirit guide. She believed that it was helpful to have as her spirit guide a man who in life had been accustomed to give commands. Napoleon was her particular favourite. She enjoyed his suave manners and charming French accent. From time to time, though, the Emperor had to fight off attempts by Viscount Nelson and the Duke of Wellington to take over his job. On one occasion, Hitler and Mussolini tried to muscle in too. I remember the Mussolini case very well. A packet of spaghetti suddenly struck me on the side of the head. Agnes blamed the Italian dictator but I saw her throw it herself.

To return to the séance in 'The Broken Staff', Agnes Mildew was simpering away at Napoleon, asking him whether he had anyone in the Beyond who wished to break the Great Silence.

'Let us have communion of the Quick and the Dead,' she cried.

Immediately, Agnes's head slumped onto her chest. Her breathing became stertorous. We all tried to follow this, as Miss Mildew had previously instructed us to do, but we sounded like nothing so much as a sextet of broken bassoons.

Agnes suddenly threw up her head, eyes still closed. 'There is a woman here!' she cried.
Silence ensued.
'It's a young woman.'
A further silence.
'She's ...'

Bill Buckley suddenly emitted a blood-curdling yell. He shot up out of his chair and stepped backwards, knocking the chair over and sending it scuttling across the floor, for he was a big and powerfully built sort of fellow. Then he folded at the knees and crumpled down like a mill chimney that had been felled by the late Fred Dibnah.

The unified breathing was shattered by various yells, screams, gasps and bronchial coughs from the assembled sitters. Everyone rose. Belinda Buckley turned on the lights. The others gathered around Mr Buckley. I ran to my computers and scanned the graphs.

Bill Buckley was out cold. I could see that. He had the delta wave pattern of a brain that was unconscious. What was most fascinating, however, was that just before he fainted – I am not afraid to use the vernacular term – the brain regions associated with vision, kinaesthetic sensations of the skin and very strong emotion had all erupted into a frenzy of electrical activity. I speak, of course, within the margins of error on my measurements. The environment, however, had remained perfectly unchanged from the control readings I took before the experiment began. All of this indicated that Bill Buckley had experienced something that to the rest of us was utterly insensible. His experience was psychogenic.

***

When he came round some minutes later, and had staggered his way to a restorative tumbler full of whisky at the bar, Mr Buckley denied that he had seen anything paranormal. His explanation was that he had felt a large sneeze coming on and in holding his breath so as not to disrupt the séance, had passed out momentarily.

This was not convincing.

Agnes Mildew was quite insensitive as usual. She offered to pay Mr Buckley £500 if he told her what he had experienced. It struck me as very significant that he refused to accept this inducement. Mrs Buckley was livid at his refusal, as the cash would have offset the cost of closing the inn for the night, but I could see that Mr Buckley derived some pleasure in resisting her peremptory commands to take it.

The scientific course in these things is to form a hypothesis and then seek evidence that will refute it. I am a keen follower of that great philosopher of science, Sir Karl Popper, on such questions. Now, I do not give much credence normally to Agnes Mildew's vapid utterances at her séances, but it did seem likely to me in this case that Agnes's announcement of the arrival of a young woman from the Beyond had somehow provoked Bill Buckley's fainting attack. The obvious course, then, was to deploy another young woman to win his confidence and extract his story from him. And that was what I did.

At the University, I have a very pretty and engaging PhD student called Anita Patel. The very next day, therefore, I returned to 'The Broken Staff' with Anita, and definitely without Agnes Mildew, to have a chat with the Buckleys about the previous night's events. We arrived at one o' clock. The inn was empty apart from old Tom Mumpus enjoying half a pint of mild.

'Ah, Mr Buckley,' I said, when Bill emerged from the cellar. 'This is my research student, Anita Patel. She's a keen psychical researcher, like me.'

'Oh?' said Bill. 'Are you a scientist too? Eh, you're not a shrink, I hope?'

'Oh, no!' said Anita, with a bright smile. 'I'm a robotics engineer!'

'Really?' said Bill, also smiling. 'I was an engineer before I got into this public house malarkey!'

'What kind of engineering?'

'Oh, gear systems, packing machines, usual run of the mill stuff.'

'Sounds like what my dad used to do,' said Anita. 'He got me interested in thinking about how to give machines emotions – to make them more efficient.'

'That sounds a bit barmy,' ventured Bill. 'How can a machine feel emotions?'

'Think of it as a stored value that determines how the machine reacts to certain patterns of experience,' said Anita. 'You've heard of neural nets?'

'Of course,' said Bill, stroking his beard.

'Well, that's how it works. The machine stores patterns of things it should like and things it should dislike. Then it responds to stimuli accordingly. Anyway, I heard that you had some pretty amazing experiences here yesterday?'

'Ecky thump!' exclaimed Bill. 'You can say that again!'

'What happened?'

'Well, I don't rightly know!'

He hesitated.

'It was like a weird dream. I just can't get it out of my head.'

'Tell me all about it!' exclaimed Anita, leaning forward, enthralled.

'I heard th'owd woman – er, Miss Mildew – say summat about a young woman turnin' up; then suddenly the whole room filled with light; and you know, it'd been as dark as a coal hole at midnight before that!'

'Séance conditions?'

'Aye. But suddenly th'ole room looked like nowt but a soccer pitch under flood lamps. And in this light, all I could see were this young woman all dressed in white, long black hair down her back.'

'Sounds amazing!'

'It was. She looked like an angel; and I felt as if I might be in heaven. Sort of at peace, you know. She just smiled at me. Then she reached out her arms and put her hands on my shoulders. I felt the pressure of her fingers on my flesh. Can you believe that? I can hardly tell you what happened next. It was like electricity flowing through my body. I just flung myself backwards – not that I wanted to get away from her, but the delight was too intense for me to bear – and I kind of, well, melted away.'

'Awesome!' said Anita.

'The question is,' said Bill, 'how do I get her back again?'

'What do you mean?'

'I have to see her again. Tell me how to get her back.'

***

Bill Buckley was not, in my judgement, a man given to telling lies or indulging in flights of fancy. He really believed that he had seen a beautiful woman who pressed her fingers into his shoulders. I was equally convinced, on the basis of analysis of data from my eco-neuro-psychological device, that this set of sensations had not made its way into his consciousness by any physical route. It was highly likely that his hallucination – for I am convinced, as a scientist, that his experience was not real – was provoked by Agnes Mildew's reference to a young woman's spirit manifesting itself at the séance. This suggestion triggered a reaction, based on an unconscious sexual complex in Mr Buckley's mind, in which his conception of the ideal woman presented itself to him as a sensory delusion. I may be a computer engineer, but I have read my Freud and Jung.

 My theoretical explanation of Mr Buckley's experience was, I am sure, along the right lines; but it did nothing to summon back to the poor man's mind the presence of the beautiful woman; which presence was vital not only for Bill's own happiness but for the prospects of any major scientific conclusions from this case.

 Much though it irked me, I realised that the only way forward was to ask Agnes Mildew to carry out another séance, in which she must ask the Emperor Napoleon for more information about the raven-haired beauty who had done so much to transform Bill Buckley's character.

 On this occasion, Belinda Buckley refused to close 'The Broken Staff' early. Mr Cropper had already published a short article on the case in the Oldham Gazette, and this alone had produced a 25% increase in takings. We were therefore compelled to wait until the inn had closed at 11 pm on the next evening before carrying out the séance.

 This time, I asked Anita Patel to join the circle too. I decided to dispense with my equipment, as a psychogenic origin for the phenomena had already been established.

What was more important was a conceptual and affective analysis of Mr Buckley's utterances, and Anita, who was quite expert in the psychological analysis of emotional states, was very well placed to do this: but only if she could get Mr Buckley to talk in the first place.

The séance went very much as before. After some banter about how the Empress Marie Louise had been a wet blanket in bed after Josephine's hot water bottle, the Emperor said that he knew exactly who the ghostly Circassian beauty was, and, what is more, where her body was buried. If Agnes Mildew cared to join him after lunch tomorrow, he would lead her to the very spot where the beautiful bones lay.

This did not seem to convey very much hard information to me. Even if the message from Napoleon were true, I couldn't see how the discovery of the bones would help Bill Buckley to see his ecstatic vision once again. I realise that some clairvoyants can hold a piece of bone and conjure up all kinds of imagery, but there was zero reason for thinking that Bill Buckley could do this – or that it would be veridical even if he could.

'Why don't you all stay overnight?' suggested Belinda Buckley.

This was not a generous invitation to stay in guest rooms. We were offered blankets and bench space. However, there was some mention of a free breakfast and lunch the next day, so I agreed to stay. I had no teaching duties and my research into connectionist architectures could wait until another time. Of course, there was no prospect of keeping Agnes Mildew away at all. Tony Cropper was also ubiquitous, with his camera and notebook, happily constructing a feature article, which involved extensive searches of the cellars with Belinda Buckley as his sole guide.

The next day, after a breakfast of sausage sandwiches and lukewarm coffee, we set out - wrapped up as best we could, for though it was a fine and clear day it was also very cold - across the moor in the wake of an ebullient Agnes Mildew.

'This is the route march dictated by Napoleon,' she cried. 'His Majesty told me that the woman we are looking for is called Amélie. She died out here on the moor while waiting for a lover who betrayed her.'

'Well,' muttered Old Tom Mumpus, who had accompanied us, 'I've lived up here for two hundred year, and I've never once heard tell o' such a tale.'

'Two hundred years?' I queried.

'Aye, me and my ancestors,' the old boy explained. 'Hast tha never heard o' folk memory, young feller?'

We came to a place where a steep-sided valley opened up around a spring that bubbled up from a grassy hillock. Agnes Mildew led us all down this steep but fairly shallow valley. It was a difficult place to walk in, as there was no footpath at all over what was unpleasantly irregular ground.

'This is the place!' cried Agnes. 'I distinctly remember the Emperor showing me this place.'

The valley had widened out a bit. She started to scrabble in a peat bed that lay just before the place where she had halted. With a cry of joy, she pulled a white skull from the dark matter.

'Amélie!' she exclaimed.

'Tha daft bugger,' exploded Tom Mumpus.

He cackled with laughter.

'That's just an owd sheep, a bit like thysen!'

The old woman blustered for a while longer but eventually conceded that the Emperor must have had one too many cognacs in the Elysian fields.

The grouped tramped to 'The Broken Staff' in rather a sullen mood.

Anita Patel and I were walking with Bill Buckley, quizzing him gently as to how he felt about this failure, when Old Tom Mumpus sidled up.

'I know more about this 'ere ghost, I reckon, than th'owd bat o'er yonder,' he said, with a grin. 'Dos' tha want to know t' tale?'

We all nodded vigorously.

'Well,' he said, 'if I'm reet, we're talking about a young woman called Emily Spicer, whose husband kept the pub in th' 1840s. They weren't what tha'd call an happily married couple. My great great grandfather reckoned that t' landlord did her in; but he had no proof o' that. Emily were a big dark good-lookin' woman, and fellers used to come from miles around just to gawp at her; but one day she vanished into t' moor and no-one ever saw her again. There's nobody knows what happened to her. But my owd grandfather, he reckoned that Emily and Ogden fell out over her little dog, which Ogden hated; and that he'd actually seen Ogden kill t' dog; and that it were just after that killing when Emily disappeared. Oh, aye, Ogden were full o' remorse for years after, and finally died o' grief. We've always said in our family, that happen th'owd devil took his secret to his grave with him, if tha sees what I mean?'

'You mean there's information in his grave?' said Bill Buckley.

'Mebbe,' said Old Tom, 'mebbe not. I'm just telling you what th'owd chap told me years ago!'

***

You can imagine that this information acted like sunflower oil on the dull fire of Bill Buckley's imagination. For what follows, I'm indebted to Anita Patel, who took careful notes of a conversation she had with Bill Buckley some days later.

It seems that the next day, Bill decided that he would break in to the grave of one Ogden Spicer, landlord of 'The Broken Staff' between the years 1832 and 1848. His first task was to locate the grave. Fortunately, Tom Mumpus had a plan of the church and churchyard that showed the location of all graves, vaults and crypts. The church was no longer in use and Mr Mumpus had been prevailed upon by the authorities, at the cost of some trifling sum per quarter, to accept the role of custodian of the premises.

Ogden Spicer had been, it seems, a fairly wealthy man, being something of a slum landlord in Oldham as well as publican of the High Top and, originally, an upland sheep farmer; and he had purchased for himself and his unmarried sisters, a vault just beneath the south side of the chancel of All Souls Church.

Bill Buckley, with Tom Mumpus's plan in hand, found the approximate location of the vault very quickly. After some scrabbling in the ground just outside of the chancel wall, and removing several large, loose clods of earth, Bill found a heavy stone that bore the single word 'Spicer'.

The stone did not prove much of an obstacle to a big burly man like Bill Buckley. Borrowing a crowbar from Mr Mumpus, who seemed extremely interested in the proceedings but unwilling to become too closely involved, Bill levered the stone loose from its base, raised it up at a slight angle, and then, grabbing it with both of his immense, shovel-like hands, pushed it up and over. He danced nimbly out of the way as the slab bounced back towards him on the turf.

Stone steps descended in front of Bill's feet into the cool darkness of a brick-lined vault that stood partly within and partly outside the line of the church. Bill took a cigarette lighter from his pocket and clicked a flame into flickering being. Watched by Tom Mumpus from the dry stone wall of the graveyard, Bill began slowly to make his way down the steps. Within a few seconds, his head had vanished completely beneath the surface of the ground.

The steps opened into a musty chamber that was about eight feet long, eight feet wide and perhaps seven feet tall. Everywhere, the flickering light picked out small red bricks. These made up the flooring, the walls and the barrel vault of the roof. A pile of four coffins was stacked up along the south wall of the vault, and two others lay separately on the ground.

Bill Buckley realised at this point that he had no clear idea of what he was looking for. Old Tom had merely conjectured that Ogden Spicer had taken a secret to the grave with him. What form could the secret possibly take? A letter? A confession? A photograph? Would it give some indication of where Amélie or Emily had gone to, or where she was to be found?

Bill glanced around the vault, seeing if it contained anything other than coffins. There was nothing else. The only obvious place to look then was in Ogden's own coffin.

Bill searched for name plates. The two coffins that lay apart had no identifying marks at all. Of the four that were stacked, he quickly found, by clambering up them like a mountain goat, that the one on top was Ogden's. He also noticed that the coffin was damaged. The case was disintegrating on one side and the inner lead lining had burst open. 'So,' thought Bill, 'Ogden Spicer were a fat pig who proved too big for his boots even in death!'

Bill shone his lighter into the cracked coffin and saw only some dry bones. This decided him. Positioning himself at the bottom of the coffin, he pulled it away from the wall until it over-balanced and came crashing down on one of the separate cases on the ground.

Ogden's case, weakened by his explosive decay many years ago, simply fell apart, and skull, ribs, pelvis, femurs, scattered in all directions. Bill knelt down, rummaging in the debris for any useful information, eagerly searching for a book, a slate, a sheet of metal, anything that might have writing or a diagram on it; but there was nothing. In exasperation and disappointment, he kicked the closest of the two separate coffins that now lay beneath Ogden's rubble.

It then struck Bill that there was something odd about these two coffins. They looked very new. What were they doing in this vault? The most recent interment was supposed to have been in 1868 but these were obviously modern pieces of work. Something was going on here. Perhaps somebody had already been investigating Emily Spicer's story and was storing what they'd discovered in these two new boxes?

Bill picked up his crowbar and applied it to the lid of the nearest coffin. To his surprise, the lid lifted up without any resistance at all. He held his cigarette lighter above the open coffin. Inside, to his astonishment, was a perfectly preserved young woman with long dark hair. She looked as if she might have breathed only a minute before.

Bill's heart began to melt as he thought that perhaps this was in fact Emily, miraculously preserved by her sheer beauty. Not even the Angel of Death would dare to destroy so magnificent a girl. And then he noticed that she was wearing jeans and a T-shirt. As he gazed at her incredulously, wondering whether he had stumbled across evidence of some bizarre cult, he noticed the girl's lips beginning to tremble, her eyes opening in uncontrollable horror, and a scream emerging from her mouth like an express train from a railway tunnel.

He leapt back with a shout, just in time for the second coffin lid to fly open and strike him on the knee. With a yelp of pain, and a mind spinning with a plenitude of possible explanations for what he had just seen, he shot up the staircase and fled into the spring sunshine and healthy fresh air as quickly as he could.

'What's the matter?' called Tom Mumpus, as Bill sped towards him across the graveyard.

Bill stopped and turned round to stare at the mouth of the vault. From it emerged two young women, one blonde and the other brunette, both unspeakably pretty, and both crying in some distress.

'Sow and ye shall reap,' remarked old Tom, with a cackle.

The two girls looked nervously at Bill and Tom. Tom called over to them, suggesting that they might like to visit his house for a cup of tea; but after no more than a single moment of indecision, they leaped over the graveyard wall and ran off across a field.

'Your idea was bloody useless,' complained Bill to Tom.

'Mebbe,' said Tom, 'but I'd been wonderin' what was going on in that churchyard.'

***

For the next part of this story, I am indebted to Chief Inspector Ian Law of the Greater Manchester Police, who provided me with a summary account of interview transcripts in his custody.

Later that day, three Russian men went into 'The Broken Staff' and found Bill Buckley up a pair of stepladders replacing a broken light bulb.

'We look for William Buckley,' they said, their eyes full of suspicion and fury.

Bill gazed at them for a moment.

'He's in the back room there, with Mrs Buckley,' he said. 'But you can't go in there.'

The Russians pushed past him, giving his ladder a shove as they went. Bill gave a yell and toppled off; but he landed on his feet and immediately sidled out of the building. He winced, though, for the blow struck to his knee by the coffin lid in the vault was now proving to be painful.

In the private back room of the inn, Tony Cropper was just giving Mrs Buckley a chaste kiss of friendship. This was to celebrate the fact that between them, by publishing the romantic story of Emily Spicer in the Oldham Gazette, they had increased the pub's takings by 50% in the last week.

They were in the middle of this osculatory exultation when the Russian called Gregor picked Mr Cropper up by the ears and flung him on to the top of the dining table. Pyotr and Sergei then proceeded to beat him about the nose and testicles, all the while shouting, 'Where are our women, Buckley?' and 'You must pay us back the cost of our investment, English grunt!' It was only when Cropper's screams had died down, due to his blacking out, that the three Russians were able to hear what Belinda Buckley was shouting at them, 'This isn't my husband!'

Sergei stopped his fists in mid flight and stared at Belinda.

'What does he look like, this William Buckley?'

'He's about so tall and has a long black beard.'

'The bastard has tricked us!' shouted Sergei.

With a last pulping of Cropper's nose, as a punishment for not telling them sooner that he was not the man they were looking for, the three Cossacks rushed out of the pub and stood by the church gate, scanning in all direction for any sign of Bill Buckley.

At quite the wrong moment, Bill, who was hiding in a peat bog about five hundred yards across the moor behind the inn, crassly chose to raise his head over a grassy hummock and peer back towards High Top hamlet.

'I see him!' cried Gregor.

With a yell, the three Russians gave chase. However, Bill knew the moor better than they did; and when they reached where he had been, they could no longer see him. They concluded that he must be running deeper into the moor via the sunken bogs, using the tussocks of grass as cover for his movements.

In the distance, Pyotr noticed a tall dark-haired woman staring at them.

'Hey,' he said, nudging Gregor. 'Is that Elena?'

'It looks like it. And where she is, the thief Buckley is likely to be too.'

The three men set a course for the dark apparition that stood before them. But as they drew closer to her, she vanished.

Then they saw Bill some four hundred yards ahead of them, jumping over a dry stone wall and disappearing from view. They pursued him stealthily this time, giving Bill no indication of their progress. When they reached the wall, they dropped to the ground behind it. Gregor peered over the top, cautiously.

'He is standing on some rocks, searching the ground,' whispered Gregor. 'He is trying to find a hiding place, a cave, or a cleft maybe.'

'Can he see us?' asked Pyotr.

'No, he has gone down, out of view,' said Gregor.

The three men rose up and vaulted over the dry stone wall. Keeping low, like commandos on a mission, they silently approached the Ladder Rocks at Standedge, where Bill Buckley had concealed himself in a small cavity.

Ladder Rocks, I should explain, is an immense outcrop of millstone grit, right at the edge of Black Peat Moor, with a panoramic vista over Marsden hundreds of feet below. In some places, huge chunks of rock litter the grassy upland as it starts to curve down; in others, cliff faces of lined and cracked rock plunge vertically down; and in yet others, pathways of stone lead out to pointing promontories with great chasms between them.

Bill probably felt quite safe in his small cave but a sudden fall of stones and small rocks on top of him must have made him panic. He bolted out of his nest right beneath the eyes of the three Russians, who spread themselves out judiciously to cut off any hope of escape. Bill had no choice but to run along a rocky ledge that led in a long curve past a series of immense boulders and out onto a spur, about ten feet wide at the start, that tapered to about one foot at the end, and which fell away in vertical drops of five hundred feet on either side.

The Russians blocked his exit. They came towards him slowly, their eyes full of calculation.

'Tell us where you have taken our girls, and we will let you go,' called Pyotr.

'I don't know anything about your girls,' shouted Bill.

'You are a liar.'

They edged closer towards him.

Bill sized the men up. They were all three much smaller than he was. The Russians could see that he was estimating his chances of throwing some of them over the side if they charged him, or, perhaps, if he charged them.

The next instant, the Russians could see that Bill was distracted. He was staring across the void to his north, looking intently at a dark-haired woman in a long white dress. This woman, who bore a remarkable resemblance to their 'property', Elena, was smiling at Bill and beckoning to him.

Surely she could not mean that he should jump over the chasm?

Immediately, the Russians felt some alarm. If Bill Buckley did jump successfully to the next spur of rock, then he might be able to escape. Taking the rocky ledge back would slow them down enough to allow Bill to conceal himself again in another cave or to go to ground in the moorland around.

One of them started to edge backwards to safeguard against this possibility. The other two stared at Bill, mesmerised by the visible signs of struggle on his face as he decided whether to leap or not.

'You know you want to!'

The woman was calling to Bill. Immediately, he drew back a few steps, and then hurled himself out over the chasm.

He did not call out as he fell to earth with an acceleration of 9.81 metres per second per second. He did not wave his arms or his legs. Gregor and Sergei watched him fall through the air. His body was swallowed up by the moorland grass.

All three Russians looked up at the dark woman. She was no longer there.

***

I'm preparing this last section of my lecture in the ruins of 'The Broken Staff'.

The poor old inn is no longer hospitable. It has only half a roof. The rest of the slates have been cracked by the heat of a fire and then lifted from the charred timbers by the cruel westerly winds that blow torrential rain across this side of the Pennines.

The windows are all smashed. The floors have been ruined by floods of water from burst pipes and smashed tanks, from the pumps of the Greater Manchester fire brigade, and finally from the driving rains that once made Lancashire the cotton capital of the world.

After Bill Buckley's death, which the coroner's jury determined was an accident, the Russians served some time in prison for the grievous bodily harm they committed on Tony Cropper, and for trafficking women into the United Kingdom for the purposes of prostitution. Then they were deported.

Mr Cropper moved in with Belinda Buckley and together they tried to make the pub a success. The sensational story that I have outlined in this monograph did indeed attract many curious people to drink and even to eat in their tavern. However, these people seldom came back more than once. This was because the place seemed to be infested with the spirit of mischief.

For instance, a man and his lady would be sitting at a table, eating their steak and kidney pudding and chips, when a wall lamp would fall off the wall above their heads with a flash and a bang, or the salt and pepper pots would suddenly topple sideways, spreading their contents across a plateful of scarcely eaten food.

Naturally, these happenings attracted a great deal of attention for a while, but visitors soon shied away when the price of a visit was a broken nose from a flying saucepan, or a drenching from a mass of water that suddenly and mysteriously fell on one's head from the ceiling.

One has to give credit to Mr Cropper and Mrs Buckley. They tried everything they could think of in order to profit from the strange happenings, including dramatic performances of 'The Strange story of Emily Spicer and Bill Buckley', played by aspiring actors from the Royal Northern College of Stage Studies, and bed-and-breakfast packages for anyone desirous of sharing mattress, pillows and bedclothes with an orgy of poltergeister. Someone even scratched love-hearts on the walls of the inn with the names of Emily and Bill surrounded by fluttering cherubs.

Naturally, Agnes Mildew took all this to be convincing evidence of personal survival and of the existence of at least platonic romance in the astral plane. She was ecstatic when a small poodle materialised out of thin air and landed on her lap. As a scientist, I am naturally more sceptical. I know that I threw the poodle.

My own theory, and again I say this in strict confidence within the circle of our own learned society, is that Mr Cropper and Mrs Buckley decided fairly quickly that the ghost story would not furnish them with a long-term revenue stream. Instead, they schemed, I am sure, to destroy the building under the specious cover of a supernatural plague of mischievous spirits. That way, they could claim a generous insurance package and start afresh somewhere else, namely, a small hotel in Cyprus.

I also think that Mr Cropper and Mrs Buckley did not have the application and intelligence to lay out a good ghost story right at the base of their spooky business at 'The Broken Staff'. What I mean is that they did not enquire sufficiently about the facts of Emily Spicer's disappearance. This is surprising, given Mr Cropper's trade as a journalist. On the other hand, it is perhaps indicative of the lamentable state into which popular journalism has fallen in this country. I appreciate that coroners' records from the nineteenth century have all too often been destroyed, and so the novice is too easily inclined to give up the chase; but in this case I was able to find the file on Emily Spicer not in the Oldham Record Office, which now covers the hamlet of High Top, but in the Huddersfield Council archives, which had had it originally from the old West Riding County Council in Wakefield.

The true story is that Emily Spicer and her husband Ogden were not very happily married. Ogden, in an effort to please his wife, bought her a small dog. This made life easier at the tavern until Ogden became increasingly irate with the dog, which was constantly under his feet, and began to kick it out of his way. Emily remonstrated with him angrily about this cruelty but Ogden took no notice. One day, the dog disappeared. In front of witnesses, Emily accused Ogden of killing it, which he denied. She, disbelieving him, stormed out of the house. She was never seen again. Her body was never discovered. However, some years later, the coroner's jury returned a verdict of accidental death on the basis of two pieces of evidence. The first was that her wedding ring was found about a year later by Ogden Spicer, to his evident surprise and distress, as attested by impartial witnesses, in the dust at the bottom of the coal shed at the back of his tavern. The second piece was that the remains of a white dress, such as Emily had been wearing, were found two years later, caught in a crevice at the bottom of Ladder Rocks. Of flesh and bone, however, there was no trace.

OUR JACK'S BACK

Frank's father had been a plumber's mate. Frank himself was a plumber; and not just any old plumber, but a master of his trade, working in gas as well as in water and waste; and he was the proud owner of a business that employed twenty two men and three women.

If Frank had one ambition left in life, it was for his son Jimmy to continue the Heap family's ascent up the ladder of occupational status, and become a fully qualified engineer; and not just any old engineer, but one with the range and impact of a Brunel; one whose profound insight into the laws of physics would lengthen the lives of folk in the 21st century.

There was, however, a basic problem in implementing this plan. Out of a sense of class loyalty, Frank had continued to live on the council housing estate where he had grown up.

You should not take this to mean that Frank was a modest man. He was, in fact, very ostentatious. He had bought a row of four council houses and had turned them into a striking, if far too linear and thus inconvenient, mansion. The problem was not so much living in a house that according to Frank's wife, Greta, was like a derailed corridor train. Rather, it was that young Jimmy, though a bright lad, had to go to Pierrepoint comprehensive school, which had the track record of an athlete with an iron ball clamped to each ankle.

Three different head-teachers had broken their careers in the daunting task of improving Pierrepoint; but since the only jobs that ever became vacant in Blackdale involved nothing more taxing than emptying and repacking boxes, very few families could see the point of aiming high and working hard at school; and the head-teachers had all given up in despair.

'You're going to have to get him into a different school,' said Greta one evening, as she and Frank ended the day with a glass of Cava each in the Jacuzzi. 'He'll never become another Brummell if you leave him at Pierrepoint.'

'Brunel,' corrected Frank.

'Oh, dear, too much fizz,' said his wife. 'Who was Brummell, anyway?'

'Some drinking buddy of the Prince Regent's,' said Frank. 'I saw it on Blackadder.'

'Whatever, we need to get Jimmy into a new school, pronto.'

It was therefore agreed among the Heaps that they would sell the tarted-up terrace and buy a smart house in the Blackdale suburb of Rakeborough. This followed logically from Greta's notion of what it was to be genteel, and gave Jimmy a right to a place at the Fusiliers' School, which, although it was still a comprehensive, drew the vast majority of its intake from the affluent middle classes, and had a distinguished record of getting young people from relatively humble backgrounds into Oxford, Cambridge and Huddersfield universities.

'You'll also be closer to Herr Sussmayr too,' said Greta to Jimmy. Heinz Sussmayr was the boy's private piano tutor and claimed to be descended from the fellow who had completed Mozart's Requiem after the great man's premature death. In Greta's book, being able to play a musical instrument was a mark of distinction. Now Jimmy would be able to nip around the corner for his lesson, rather than have to take a thirty minute car ride through the perpetual gridlock of Blackdale town centre.

Frank, for his part, hoped that the move to Fusiliers from Pierrepoint would put an end to Jimmy learning more about physics from his Dad and a Meccano set than from science teachers.

'Water-hammer,' said Frank to Jimmy one day, in a reflective mood. 'That's what you need to get them to teach you. It's the plumber's biggest headache. It sounds weird, but what causes water-hammer is one of the hardest problems yet to be solved in mathematics. Navier-Stokes, it's called. You'll make your name if you solve that one, lad. Look it up on Wikipedia.'

The new house was an imposing, three-storey, detached building, made up of alarmingly large square stones. It stood beneath the craggy summit of Blackrock Edge, half way up the winding road that crosses the Pennine moors into Yorkshire. It had a central front door and symmetrically arranged windows. From the spacious entrance hall, doors led into a drawing room, a dining room, a study that Frank decided to use as his office, and a kitchen. An elegant staircase ran up to a landing from which one could enter four bedrooms, one en suite, and a large communal bathroom. The stairs continued up into a spacious attic with three dormer windows at the front and another three at the back. This floor would doubtless have accommodated servants at one time but was now given over to a small storage room, a further bathroom, and a large open space.

Frank and Greta decided that the huge attic space should be a rumpus room for Jimmy. What their notion of rumpus was is indicated by the fact that for the boy's thirteenth birthday, they bought him a baby grand piano and had it hauled up to this room. That way, they said, he could practise his scales and arpeggios in style.

Frank and Greta left the old upright piano where it had been, standing along a wall of the attic. They thought they might move it elsewhere in the house later.

Greta was proud of Edge House. She described it, with historical if not quite architectural accuracy, as Upland Georgian. She bought a grandfather clock for the hall, read all about Beau Brummell on Google and started to tour the auction rooms of Lancashire and Cheshire in search of Georgian and Regency furnishings that might give the house a sympathetic interior.

Frank was pleased with the solid yet neat style of the building. He congratulated himself on knowing a good pile of masonry when he saw one. He had been able to get the place for a cracking price. And yet the only defect that he could detect in its structure and services was, ironically enough, a tendency towards water-hammer in the pipes. And that, at least, could be turned to didactic purposes for young Jimmy.

The one thing that Frank was not so pleased about was that he no longer felt distinctive. To be sure, he lived in a grand house, but 'so did every other bugger' thereabouts. Nobody would gaze at Edge House and say, 'Bloody hell, them Heaps 'ave done 'emselves proud,' since to all the people who lived in Rakeborough, Edge House seemed pretty normal.

Greta's delight in her new home was slightly tarnished by the fact that she felt a little out of place among the smart folk of the village. She had an uneasy feeling that the many lawyers and doctors who lived there looked down, secretly, on her and her family. But she was an optimistic woman, and knew that she would eventually find some way of asserting her social equality.

'Have you seen that old codger who keeps starin' at the house?' she asked Frank one day, after tea.

'You mean the bloke with the white moustache and little dog?'

'That's the one. He makes me feel as if I were in a bleedin' zoo!'

'Ah, just ignore him.'

The sound of Jimmy thumping out *Twinkle, twinkle, little star* on the baby grand piano echoed down from the loft.

'Do you think he's happy in his new school?'

'I reckon so,' said Greta. 'He's struggling with the homework a bit; but the boys like him because he's a good goalie; and he doesn't complain if they leave him there for a whole match!'

'What's he playin' this baby music for?'

'It's proper piano music, not a nursery rhyme. Herr Sussmayr set it for him.'

'A wind chime 'd play it better than he does.'

'Don't be mean. At least he's trying.'

***

A few weeks after the Heaps had moved into Edge House, the postman could not fit a parcel through their letter box. Getting no reply to his knock, he left a note asking them to pick it up from the post office in Rakeborough. Greta called for it one morning on her way back from the Co-op.

'Ah, yes, it's just here,' said the lady behind the desk.

She opened a cupboard door and took out the packet.

'Here you are.'

'Oh, thanks very much. Oh, it's for my son, Jimmy.'

Without a thought, Greta opened the packet.

'Oh,' she said. 'It's a book. Heath Robinson's *Absurdities*. I didn't know Jimmy was interested in this kind of thing!'

The book was full of drawings of strange and comical contraptions. One showed an elaborate system of strings and pulleys to pour water on serenading cats.

'I can think of worse things for boys to be interested in!'

'You're right, there!'

'You must be the new people up at Edge House?'

'We are.'

'How do you like it up on the hill?'

'It's lovely. What a beautiful old house.'

'No problems then?'

'No. Should there be?'

'No, no, – but you know what these old houses are like.'

'The only thing that bothers me is an old man who keeps coming and staring at the bloody place.'

'A tall man with a little dog?'

'Yes.'

'That'll be old Mr Schofield. Don't mind him. He's a nice man, really.'

'Who is he, then?'

'Oh, he used to live there years ago. In the 1930s, I think.'

'Well, I'm surprised he didn't buy it back when it came on the market, if he loves the place so much.'

The clerk shrugged.

'Well, I must get on,' said Greta. 'I've a flower arranging class to go to.'

'Very nice to meet you,' replied the clerk.

***

When she got back home from her class, Greta again saw Mr Schofield gazing at the house. His little dog was glaring at a dormer window in the attic and barking furiously. Greta pulled into the drive with intention of speaking to the old fellow; but even though she emerged from the car twice as quickly as normal, he had already scuttled off down the hill towards the village.

Greta unlocked the front door and went straight up to the attic. Jimmy was sitting quietly at his desk. She ruffled his hair and put her hands on his shoulders.

'Didn't you hear that dog barking, Jimmy?' she asked. 'It was jumping up here like there was a string of sausages hanging out of the window. Were you taunting it, or something?'

'I was doing my homework.'

He showed her his exercise book.

'What are you doing?'

'Something about electrical circuits.'

'Now, you do understand it, don't you?'

'Most of it.'

'Well, your Dad'll saw your leg off if you mess it up again this time.'

Greta went away again, humming 'All you need is love.'

Jimmy was trying to work out how to calculate total resistance when resistors are arranged in both series and parallel. Series was easy; but he could not really understand why the parallel rule worked as it did; and so he could never remember how to do it. When he had to calculate the combined resistance of a circuit that included both, he floundered.

He was trying to figure out what he had to do when he heard a girl's voice whispering to him: 'Work out the parallel bit first; then add that to the other two bits in series.'

Jimmy looked around him in astonishment. He tapped his laptop to see if anyone was talking to him over the internet.

'Hello?' he said.

There was no answer.

He continued to work.

The whisper returned: 'Not like that.'

Jimmy got up and searched the whole attic thoroughly. Again, there was nobody there. This was odd but Jimmy was an unimaginative lad and he focused on the practical issue, which was that the voices were helping him crack a difficult science problem. They were friendly, so why be afraid of them?

Jimmy worked out the combined resistance of the parallel resistors first.

'Good boy. Now add that number to the two others in series.'

Jimmy did what he was told.

'We're going to like you, Jimmy,' said a deeper whisper, an older boy's voice.

Jimmy scratched his head and covered up the webcam on his laptop, just in case some other kids were spying on him over the internet.

***

Frank was out jogging one evening when he almost stumbled over Mr Schofield and his dog. He ground to a halt and, panting, said, 'You're Mr Schofield.'

The old man looked rather startled but did not attempt to run away. He merely nodded.

'Can I do anything for you, mate?' asked Frank.

'I'm sorry?'

'I wondered why you stand staring at our house so much?'

'I don't mean to be rude. I used to live there, you see.'

'I know. Someone told my wife.'

'I haven't been in the house since 1937.'

'Do you want to come in and have a look around?'

'Oh, no, no. Not at all. I wouldn't want to disturb you.'

'We wouldn't mind.'

'No, thank you all the same. My memories of Edge House aren't very happy.'

'Are you sure?'

'Yes.'

'Well, I'll see you around, I expect.'

***

A few days later, Jimmy came home and proudly showed his Mum that he had won an A grade for his science homework.

'Good lad,' she said, kissing him on his forehead. 'Your Dad'll be pleased. Now go and practise your piano.'

'I will', said Jimmy, 'but do we have a valve radio?'

'Eh?'

'You know, an old wireless, with glass vacuum valves rather than transistors.'

'What on earth do you want one of them for?'

'Somebody told me that music sounds better on them.'

'Who?'

'Just a friend.'

'Your Grandad might have one, I suppose.'

Jimmy went to see his Grandad Heap, who rummaged in the pantry beneath his staircase and triumphantly brought out an ancient Bush wireless set that had been stored there for the last thirty years. It was one of the classic 1930s 'Cathedral' sets and had originally belonged to old Mr Heap's mother and father. Jimmy took the wireless home on the bus. Back in his attic, he connected the old radio to his laptop using an earphone jack with its wires cut open, so that the laptop could play through the valves and mellow loudspeaker.

***

What Jimmy had been playing on the piano a few days earlier had not been the nursery rhyme 'Twinkle, twinkle, little star', but a simplified version of Mozart's twelve variations on that tune, called 'Ah, vous dirai-je, Maman'. This was, and still is, a popular melody for beginners to learn and practise. Jimmy was then certainly no more than a beginner, despite two years' worth of lessons from Herr Sussmayr.

Jimmy was painfully trying to get his fingers to the right places on the keyboard to play the easy version when the same disembodied girl's voice whispered, just behind his left ear, 'Close your eyes and imagine your fingers flying over the keys.'

Jimmy glanced over his shoulder. The hairs on the back of his head began to bristle slightly. He instantly calculated his options.

He had no idea where the voice was coming from but understood that it would help him to do things. He also sensed that there would be a price to pay; and though he did not know what that price would be, he wondered whether it could ever be worth paying.

On the other hand, he wanted to impress his mother with his piano playing just as he had recently pleased his father with his command of the laws of physics. Happen the voice was only that of his own imagination? He'd seen on the telly that you could achieve great things if you relaxed and let your subconscious mind speak to you.

'Let me move your fingers,' whispered the girl.

Jimmy thought of his cringing father and of the scoldings of Herr Sussmayr.

'Relax and let me guide your hands.'

Jimmy relaxed.

'Close your eyes,' whispered the voice.

To his astonishment, Jimmy, with his mind in darkness, heard his fingers pressing the right keys and, what is more, at the right times. He could suddenly play the simplified piece with great ease and fluency.

Jimmy got up from the piano and went to his laptop. Finding an online copy of the full score of the twelve variations, he downloaded it and printed it off there and then. Returning to the keyboard, he started to play the full piece. The passages he had not practised before were not yet brilliant to his touch but he could find his way to the end of each variation without falling into an abyss. And the next time he played the variation through, the better his rendition sounded.

Down in the kitchen, Frank and Greta were blending soup. Every time the blender stopped, they could hear Jimmy playing something yet more elegant and embellished. They eventually left the soup behind and crept up to the first floor landing to listen.

'It must be a professional recording,' said Frank.

'It sounds real to me.'

They stealthily mounted the stairs to the attic and from the penultimate step watched Jimmy's fingers caress the keys, eyes closed in what appeared to be a rhapsody as the most delicate music flowed out of his body.

***

One day, Greta was in the post office buying stamps when Mr Schofield came in. She saw him as she turned to go.

'You're Mr Schofield, aren't you?'

He looked as if he'd rather run away than answer, but gave her a weak smile.

'I am.'

'Hello. I'm Greta Heap. I live in Edge House.'

She held out her hand.

Mr Schofield smiled nervously.

'I've seen you around,' he said, holding out his own. 'Jack Schofield.'

They shook hands.

'You used to live in our house?'

'Oh, I did, years ago,' said Mr Schofield.

'You should pay us a visit and see the old place.'

'Oh, no, I mustn't make a nuisance of myself.'

He coughed violently and, waving his hands apologetically, slipped out of the post office without asking for anything.

'That's odd,' said Greta. 'Does he think I'm a man-eater or something?'

'Oh, I don't think it's you, love,' said the shop keeper. 'He's scared of the house.'

'What do you mean?'

'Well, I don't know the full story, but there was a terrible accident at the house when he was a young boy, and he hasn't been back since.'

'What kind of accident?'

'I don't know the details, but his older brother and sister were killed somehow.'

'How?'

'All I know is that it was an accident.'

***

Jimmy, having allowed the whispering voices to aid his brain and his fingers, decided that he would allow them to unlock his potential in lots of different areas. The boy's voice seemed keen to help with mathematics in particular. It was not long before Jimmy understood not only the elements of algebra, but also how to solve simultaneous and quadratic equations, and even the basics of the differential calculus. At first, his teachers suspected cheating; but the boy performed just as well under examination conditions. Plaudits soon began to wing their way to Edge House from Fusiliers School at this astonishing emergence of a Newton *redivivus*.

A few evenings later, Frank returned to Edge House after jogging and again found Jack Schofield gazing at the house. He was studying the windows of Jimmy's attic again. This time, the dog was not barking but was lying contentedly beside its master's feet. Jack appeared to be listening to Jimmy playing 'Ah, vous dirai-je, Maman' on his grand piano.

'Enjoying the music, Mr Schofield?' asked Frank.

'The lad plays well.'

'He's got much better since being here. It must be the fresh air.'

'It's good to hear music again coming from the old house.'

'Did you used to play?'

'Oh, a little; but I wasn't a patch on my brother and sister.'

'Jimmy seems to be getting better and better every day.'

The front door opened and Greta appeared.

'Hello, Mr Schofield,' she said. 'And how are you?'

'I'm fine, thank you. I was just praising your son's facility at the piano.'

'And he's getting much better at his maths and science too,' smiled Greta, 'which pleases Frank, as he's keen for his little lad to become an engineer.'

'I was an engineer once.'

'Really? What kind?' asked Frank.

'Mechanical.'

'That's the ticket. I keep telling Jimmy that he has to get into fluid flow.'

'That's a very arcane field.'

'He could make a fortune if he solved the Navier-Stokes equations.'

'Good Lord! You're ambitious.'

'Well, he could begin by sorting out water-hammer, starting with this house. It's like having a poltergeist here sometimes.'

Jack Schofield smiled thinly.

'Oh, you and your equations,' complained Greta. 'Would you like a cup of tea, Mr Schofield?'

'Tea?' said Jack, going very pale. 'No, not tea. I'm sorry.'

'Well, coffee then?'

'Oh, I don't know.'

His watery eyes darted from one to the other.

'Go on,' said Frank. 'I know you're dying of curiosity to see the inside of the house!'

There was a moment's silence.

'Oh, very well,' said Jack. 'Just a quick look round.'

Greta took Jack's arm and, with the garrulous charm that made her so attractive to older men, led him into the drawing room indoors. She chatted while Frank attended to the coffee pot.

'So when did you leave Edge House?' asked Greta.

'It was 1937.'

'And where did you go to?'

'Not far away. We moved into Roman Farm. My father let Edge House to various tenants but none of them stayed very long.'

'Why was that?' cried Greta. 'I can't understand it. It's such a lovely house.'

'I found it a bit oppressive myself,' said Jack. 'I had to move away.'

'Oh, I understand,' said Greta, squeezing his arm gently. 'You have unhappy memories.'

Jack nodded.

'Edward and Mary were both very clever. Edward was quite a mathematician and Mary was a musical genius.'

'There was some kind of accident?'

Jack took a handkerchief from his jacket pocket and blew his nose.

'Yes,' he said, and then paused, obviously wondering what to say. 'I was a much more practical boy. I was interested in engineering. I was always fiddling around with engines of one sort or another. I volunteered for the RAF as soon as I turned eighteen – the War was on then, of course – and after a few tests and a training course I was assigned to a Lancaster bomber crew as an engineer. Despite the danger, I loved that job, keeping that beautiful aircraft in the sky.'

'That must have been so scary!'

'It was – especially when I was shot down over Germany.'

'Really?'

'Yes, though I was too busy to be scared right then.'

'What happened?'

'Flak took out three of our engines over Hamburg. We had to limp along the coast and bail out. I was almost shot by Nazi sentries several times, but managed to sneak on board a Swedish steamer and make it to neutral territory. From Sweden, I got back to Britain by the air shuttle to RAF Leuchars in Scotland. After debriefing, I was given leave and came to Blackdale for a few weeks. But when I got here, I found that my girlfriend had just been killed by a stray V1 flying bomb. That upset me more than my own brush with death at Hamburg. I went back to night bombing and was lucky enough to survive the war. After that, I taught engineering to mechanics students at technical college, and then became a school teacher of physics. I never married, as nobody else seemed to live up to my poor Doreen. And here I am now, an old man who lives in his memories - and most of those are pretty unpleasant.'

'What a sad story,' commented Greta.

'Believe me, it could be worse.'

Upstairs, Jimmy whistled. Jack's dog jumped up and ran out of the drawing room and up the stairs.

'Oh, Nifty, come back here!' cried Jack in dismay.

'I'll go and get him for you,' said Frank.

'You should go up yourself, Mr Schofield, and see Jimmy's lovely new piano,' suggested Greta. 'It's a baby grand.'

'I think that would be too much for me,' said Jack.

'Oh, is that where ...'

Jack nodded.

'It's funny how Nifty used to bark so much at the house, but now he seems quite happy with the place,' said Greta.

'Something's obviously changed here,' murmured Jack.

Jack stared at the empty fireplace in silence for a few moments.

Frank reappeared.

'I can't get the dog to come down,' he said. 'And I don't fancy picking him up. He growls whenever I move my hands towards him. He seems to like being with Jimmy.'

'It looks like you'll have to go up, after all,' said Greta to Jack. 'Are you alright with that?'

Jack grimaced but rose from his chair. He went up the stairs, followed by Greta and Frank in procession. In silence, they passed over the first landing, and continued up the narrow steps to the loft.

The door into Jimmy's rumpus room was open. Jimmy and Nifty were standing in line just inside it like a welcoming party.

'Mr Schofield!' said Jimmy, with a thin smile. 'Welcome back after so many years!'

Frank looked at his son in amazement.

'Here's the piano,' twittered Greta.

Jack looked solemnly around the room before resting his eyes on the grand.

'It's a fine instrument,' he said, at last. 'What have you been playing, Jimmy?'

'Mozart, mainly,' said the boy. 'I've found out that I love his strange combination of sadness and sweetness. It never cloys.'

Frank grinned and scratched his head.

'Do you have any particular piece that's your favourite?'

'There is one I'd like to play,' said Jimmy. 'But ...'

'But what?'

'I need your help.'

'Why?'

'It requires two pianists.'

'Can't one of your parents play?'

'No.'

'What is the piece?'

'K448.'

Jack turned pale. Greta thought that he might faint.

'I know it,' he muttered.

'You used to play it?' said Jimmy.

Jack nodded.

'With Mary, sometimes.'

'Play it with me now,' urged Jimmy.

Jack shook his head.

'I can't,' he said. 'I was never as good as Mary.'

'You'll be good enough for me, I'm sure.'

'It's years since I played anything.'

'Oh, do play, Mr Schofield,' urged Greta.

Jimmy sat down at the grand piano and pointed to the old pianoforte along the wall.

'Come on,' he said. 'You can do it.'

Jack sat down in front of the upright, beads of sweat forming on his brow.

Jimmy smoothed the music out on the stand.

'I'll take the first part,' he said. 'You take the second.'

'That sounds so familiar,' muttered Jack.

'I'll count us in. One, two, three, four.'

Man and boy started to play in perfect synchrony; but within the space of twelve bars, Jack was beginning to struggle; he was falling behind; he was losing the beat; he was hitting the wrong notes; and by the twentieth measure, he threw his hands up in despair and rose from the pianoforte.

Jimmy shrieked with laughter. He leaped up from his piano stool, strode over to Jack, clapped him on the back, and, taking a remote control from his pocket, pressed a button.

Immediately, the Bush wireless set blared out the opening of the old Jack Hylton song, 'Our Jack's Back', followed by the insinuating voice of the vocalist Leslie Sarony singing how he'd *lots of things to tell you now that our Jack's back: when he was a boy at school, sometimes he would play the fool; but the master used to break his rule - on our Jack's back!*

While this insolent song filled the room, Jack backed away in horror to the top of the stairs, his left hand fumbling for support from the table that stood beside the wall. He almost stumbled over the book *Absurdities*, the book of drawings by Heath Robinson that Jimmy had ordered a few weeks earlier, which lay on the top step. Jack looked at the title and groaned.

Jack hurried down the stairs, pursued by Nifty.

***

Afterwards, Jimmy became morose for a week. He ignored his school work and was admonished by his disappointed teachers. At home, he wandered around the house, reading boys' comics and never once touching his piano. In fact, he seldom went into the attic at all.

Greta came downstairs one day and asked Jimmy if he was learning Latin.

'No,' he said. 'Why?'

'You've written some Latin on your whiteboard up in the loft.'

'I haven't.'

'Well, it's your writing.'

'Show me.'

Mother and son traipsed back upstairs. Greta pointed the words out to Jimmy:

Hic quoque ingens bellum civile commovit.

'What does it mean?' she asked.

'I don't know,' he said.

'It's your writing, isn't it?'

'Well, yes, but I don't think I wrote it.'

'You must have.'

Jimmy shrugged his shoulders. His mother could not decide whether she was more annoyed or puzzled. She chose to say nothing and stomped off downstairs.

'*He* stirred up this civil war,' whispered the boy's voice in Jimmy's ear.

***

The next day, Jimmy asked his Dad if he could buy a model boiler and steam engine.

'Well, I suppose so,' said Frank, 'though I wish you were interested in a modern technology rather than steam. Like plasma flow, for instance.'

'Plasma flow? Is that something to do with telly screens?'

'Nuclear fusion,' replied Frank. 'A controlled fusion reactor would provide us with an unlimited source of clean energy forever. Just think of the fame you'd win if you built it, lad.'

'Thing is,' said Jimmy, 'I can't very well build a nuclear reactor in our house, can I?'

'No, I suppose not.'

'And at least I'd learn about good engineering by studying a steam system.'

'You would.'

'After all, thermodynamics was invented because of steam engines.'

'So it was. Clever lad. What kind of engine do you want?'

Father and son looked at various websites until they found a boiler and engine that Jimmy fancied. The boiler ran off bottled gas and stood about a foot high with a cylinder diameter of six inches. A brass pipe connected the boiler to a steam engine of similar size. The engine pushed a piston that drove a flywheel which in turn could deliver power to a range of machines.

'What do you want the engine to drive?' asked Frank, once the far from cheap purchase had been made with his credit card.

'I thought it might be fun to make a signalling system.'

'Signalling what?'

'Oh, any message that takes my fancy.'

'Eh?'

'It doesn't really matter, as long as it turns something.'

'You'd do well to experiment with different loads on the engine, and see what happens to steam pressure and flywheel speed.'

'I could do anything with it, really, Dad.'

'That's the spirit.'

***

When the machinery arrived, Jimmy and Frank were ready and waiting with the bottle of propane gas. Within an hour, they had assembled the system and were getting up steam.

Jimmy had already designed and built an apparatus by which a cog, driven by a band from the flywheel, moved a message board out of some housing, around a cigar-shaped track and back into the housing again. As the engine came up to pressure, he gave the flywheel a nudge. It began to turn; and the traction system dragged out into the open a message board which said: 'Thanks for the steam engine, Dad!'

Frank laughed boisterously and clapped his son on the back. Still laughing, he ran off downstairs to tell Greta about Jimmy's witty display.

Jimmy turned off the gas. He looked with satisfaction at the machinery in front of him. With the length of copper piping, tinsnips, propane torch, flux and solder that he had stolen from his father's depot, and hidden from both his parents, he now had everything he needed.

***

Jimmy was playing with a yoyo in the front garden of Edge House, waiting for Jack Schofield to come by, as he knew Jack would. Jack always walked past the house around four o' clock in the afternoon.

As soon as Jimmy caught sight of the old man toiling up the hill, he hid himself behind one of the stone pillars of the garden gate and waited.

'Why, Mr Schofield,' he said, stepping into view as Jack drew level.

'Ah, Jimmy. How are you?'

'I'm very well, thank you. Do you have some time to spare today?'

'Why do you ask?'

'I've a little engineering project I'd like to show you.'

'Does that mean going into the attic again?'

'I'm afraid it does.'

Mr Schofield peered into Jimmy's eyes. Jimmy noticed that the old man was swallowing nervously, repeatedly.

'I'd like to help you, Jimmy, really I would; so yes, I'll come.'

'That's fantastic.'

'Where are your parents?'

'They're at the bottom of the back garden, trying to get a water feature to work properly.'

'I'd better leave Nifty here, I think.'

'You can loop his lead around the gate.'

The old man and the young boy went in through the front door and took the stairs up to the attic. When they reached Jimmy's big room, Jack could see a boiler, a steam engine, and a cigar-shaped traction device sitting in the middle of the room, with a single chair placed in front of the machinery. The boiler was rattling away on its chassis but the engine was not turning.

Jack faltered.

'What is this?'

'Would you sit in the chair and make sure the boiler doesn't go out?'

Jack glanced at Jimmy but did not sit down. Instead, he put his finger on the toothed chain for the message board and pulled the board out of its housing.

The board said: 'Everything stops for tea!'

Jimmy burst out laughing. As the grandfather clock in the hall downstairs chimed four, the Cathedral wireless set erupted into song. Edward Molloy was crooning the 1935 hit: *There isn't any war when the clock strikes four - Everything stops for tea!*

Jack sank miserably into the chair. He stared for a moment at the laughing Jimmy. Then he sprang up, seized the chair, raised it up high, and struck Jimmy over the head with it.

The boy staggered. Jack caught him before he could fall over and half frog marched, half dragged him to the small attic bathroom. He turned on both the hot and the cold taps in the sink and waited until water was flowing over the edges. Then he plunged the boy's head, face down, into the water.

A moment later, he pulled Jimmy out again.

'Hold your breath,' he commanded. 'Don't breathe the water.'

He plunged the lad back under the surface.

Jimmy tried to scream, losing some of his air in wasted bubbles. He struggled in a futile attempt to force Jack to let go of him. The old man was tall and still strong for his years. Decades of physical exercise had left him with a lean and powerful physique.

'Wash him clean,' muttered Jack, keeping a firm grip on Jimmy.

Jack monitored Jimmy's movements in minute detail, calculating, judging.

But still he held him under the water.

***

Down in the kitchen, Frank turned on the tap to fill the kettle for a cup of tea. Immediately, the house was filled with the hideous rhythmic banging and shrieking of water-hammer.

'What's causing that?' muttered Frank.

He turned the tap off.

The thumping died down but did not stop fully.

Frank turned on the tap again. The groaning and shrieking resumed. Hammer blows as of a giant at a forge resounded throughout the house. He closed the tap.

'Jimmy,' he shouted from the bottom of the stairs. 'Are you running water?'

There was no answer. Frank thought he could hear water splashing somewhere. He went upstairs, checking the bathrooms on the first floor first, and then making his way up to the attic.

He was only half way up the attic steps when he realised something was seriously wrong.

He dashed into the small bathroom just as Jimmy was losing consciousness. He could see his son's body give up the struggle and go limp.

'I'm ready if you are,' shouted Jack, his eyes raised and apparently fixed on the ceiling.

'You mad bastard!' screamed Frank.

Frank grabbed hold of Jack and spun him round to punch him in the face. Jimmy slumped to the floor, unconscious. Frank divided his attention for a moment between his son and the old man. Jack took the opportunity to dart out of the room.

Jimmy was still breathing. Frank laid his boy in the recovery position, took out his mobile phone, and called an ambulance.

While he was talking to control, Frank could hear Jack groaning in the big room. When the call was over, he glanced at Jimmy and then went out to confront the old man.

Jack was standing by the steam engine, his right foot resting on the boiler. He looked up and grimaced at Frank.

'You'll thank me yet,' he said.

Frank made a move to punch Jack. The old man drew back his foot and kicked the boiler with all the force that he could muster. The brass pipe connecting the boiler to the engine twisted and snapped. Steam hissed fiercely in a fine jet that struck Jack straight in the face.

Jack screamed. He flung up his hands to protect his eyes; but his face and hands were badly scalded. He fell to the floor and passed out as the propane burner that had fuelled the boiler turned onto its side and ignited a pile of books and papers on the fleecy rug beside Jimmy's sofa.

'Bloody hell,' muttered Frank, looking around him.

He ran back into the bathroom and filled the waste bin with water. But by the time he got back to the fire, the rug and sofa were ablaze too.

Frank dragged Jack away from the fire. Then he rushed back to Jimmy, picked the boy up in his arms, and staggered down the stairs to safety.

As soon as Jimmy and Greta were out of the house, Frank ran back up to the attic to pull Jack clear of the fire. But the smoke was already too acrid and thick. All he could do was stagger downstairs, coughing and retching, and call the fire brigade.

***

Jimmy lived. Jack died.

The undertaker commented to Frank that despite the horrific circumstances in which he had perished, Jack looked happy. Frank commented to the undertaker that Jimmy was unhappy. He had been torn apart by fear and reduced intellectually to the far from golden mean.

Edge House looked distinctly miserable. The attic and roof had been destroyed. The first floor was badly fire damaged. The whole house had been drenched with water. Without the expenditure of many thousands of pounds, it would not be inhabitable.

The Heap family were trying to make sense of events as they recovered in their rented accommodation.

'I was right first time, when I thought Schofield was a creep,' said Greta.

'I'm not so sure,' said Frank.

'But he tried to drown our Jimmy!'

'Did he, Jimmy?'

'You saw what he did,' said the boy.

'I did. It looked very nasty.'
'He just turned on me.'
'But you'd been quite unpleasant to him.'
'Frank!' protested Greta.
'Jimmy isn't normally rude. His character changed when we went to Edge House.'
'Well, that's true, I suppose,' said Greta.
'I'm still the same person,' observed Jimmy.
'No, you've lost your flair for music and maths,' said Frank.
'I was brain damaged when Schofield tried to drown me.'
'That's not what the medics say.'
'I thought I was going to die.'
'There's more to this than meets the eye,' murmured Frank.

***

The lady in the post office shook her head as Greta finished recounting the story of what had happened between Jimmy and Jack Schofield.

'Incredible,' she said. 'It's absolutely astonishing. Who could have thought that Mr Schofield would do anything like that?'

'You've no idea how his brother and sister died?'

'Only that it was an accident. But I was talking about this to the Vicar's wife the other day, and she said that Mrs Walkden might know.'

'Who's Mrs Walkden?'

'A very old lady who lives in the retirement home by the lake. She must be in her nineties by now. She was the maid at Edge House when the Schofield children died in 1936.'

'Is she still "with it", do you know?'

'Oh, yes, apparently so. She's physically quite frail, and blind; but she knows her onions still.'

***

Mrs Walkden rubbed her thumbs together as she listened to the story of what had happened to Jack Schofield.

'Oh, they were wicked, Edward and Mary,' she said. 'They used to drive poor Jack wild. They loved nothing more than to humiliate him; and they made his life a misery.'

'They tormented him?' asked Greta.

'Oh, aye, they did that. He just couldn't keep up with 'em, poor lad. That's why.'

'He wasn't as bright as they were?'

'He were clever, in his way. A practical lad, making things wi' his own hands. But they used to laugh at him and say he were an oily rag.'

'How did Edward and Mary die?'

'Jack was trying to impress them. He'd set up a little steam engine in th' attic that was going to wave semaphore flags or some such thing. But it all blew up in their faces.'

'What happened?'

'Like I say, th' engine blew up. Oh, it was horrible. There were blood everywhere.'

'How come the engine exploded?' asked Frank.

'I don't know. Coroner said there must a' been some weakness in t' metal.'

'But Jack was unhurt?'

'Nay, he were making a pot o' tea. It were tea time, you see. Eddy and Mary were kneeling right in front o' th' engine, laughing at it, when it blew shards o' metal into their throats.'

Mrs Walkden sniffed a bit and wiped her eyes. Greta squeezed the old lady's arm.

'They always made Jack make tea for 'em,' she said. 'They were rotten to him.'

'Was Jack a nice lad, then?'

'I thought so. He were kinder than they were. Less off a show off.'

'What happened after the accident?'

'Oh, Jack were in a terrible state. His mother and father were grief stricken, as any parent would be. But Jack seemed haunted by what had happened. I could hear him, walking around an' around in th' attic, muttering an' mumbling to himself.'

'You had a room in the attic?'

'I did. I'd never liked it up there much, because Edward and Mary used to wake me up in the middle o' the night sometimes with their piano music. They could be so inconsiderate. But after they'd gone for a Burton, the place got worse.'

'How?'

'For one thing, I couldn't get the memory of all that blood out of my head. It were me as what had to scrub it all up, you know, and I just could not get the stains out o' t' boards. In the end, owd Mr Schofield had joiners put a new floor put down. But worse than that, I had such bad dreams up there. I always dreamt that Mary were tryin' to touch me.'

Mrs Walkden shivered.

'We didn't stay there much longer, as it happened. Mr and Mrs Schofield couldn't bear to step foot in th' attic at all; and young Jack had what you'd call a nervous breakdown. So we all moved out, to Roman Farm, a bit further down th' hill from Blackrock Edge.'

'What happened to Edge House after that?' asked Greta.

'It changed hands a lot,' said Frank. 'I can see that from the deeds.'

'You're right there,' said the old lady. 'Nobody could settle for long.'

'Why not? Because of the accident?'

'Well, local folk knew o' that history,' said Mrs Walkden. 'But even newcomers didn't take to t' place. There were lots o' talk about t' wind making eerie whispers in th' attic. I guess that t' new flooring must a' set up some kind of fluting up there.'

'We bought the house from a property company' said Frank.

'Aye, there were lots o' tenants. None of 'em stayed very long.'

***

Edge House was ruined. Frank could not decide whether to rebuild the first and second floors, or to use the insurance money to buy a new property.

He drove up to the house one quiet Sunday morning to inspect the damage for the tenth time and finally to decide what to do. It was a bright early autumnal day. The sky was a beautiful shade of blue, giving Frank a sense of hope. Small fair weather clouds drifted across the sky in a way that infused contentment into his soul. The stone crags of Blackrock Edge high above him drew his eyes up to the glory of the Pennine landscape. The only sound he could hear was the song of a distant skylark.

Frank unlocked the front door of the house and checked that everything was in order on the ground floor. There had been no intruders. He went up the stairs and moved the chipboards and plastic sheeting that now blocked off the second floor, protecting the downstairs rooms from the bad weather to which the upper stories were now open. He manoeuvred himself past these boards and stepped onto the second floor landing.

The walls were blackened at the top and streaked with water stains. The landing stank of burned wood. Vast holes in the ceiling revealed the charred roof timbers up above and beyond them, expanses of blue sky. Although the ground floor was in reasonably good order, it would undoubtedly take a pile of cash to restore the top part of the house to life.

Warily, Frank climbed the steps up to the attic. The fire damage here was so bad that he did not dare go all the way up to the burned beams of the loft floor. The half dozen steps at the top of the staircase looked like nothing so much as bits of biscuit that would crumble if he stood on them. He had to make do with poking his head up into the attic space, keeping his feet on the last solid step.

Frank glanced around the ruined space. This could be made into a lovely open bedroom for Greta and himself. Jimmy, for whom this part of the house would obviously evoke painful memories for years to come, need not go up there. Jimmy could have a wonderful suite of rooms on the second floor. And the marvellous views from the dormer windows, up to Blackrock Edge on one side, and across the valley to Rossendale Moor on the other, would thrill Greta.

But Frank was still undecided. Pursing his lips as he thought about his options, he turned around to start going back down the brittle staircase. He was half way through his first step when he heard a girl's voice, just above his head, say softly, 'Please don't go.'

Frank spun back on his toes and looked into the roof space. There was absolutely nobody there. In that instant, Frank decided to let the house go to ruin. And in the same instant, the step on which he was standing gave way. The plumber plumbed the depths.

Printed in Great Britain
by Amazon.co.uk, Ltd.,
Marston Gate.